# FRANK ON A
# GUN-BOAT

## HARRY CASTLEMON

1st WORLD
LIBRARY
Literary Society

# Frank on a Gun-Boat

## Harry Castlemon

© 1st World Library – Literary Society, 2006
PO Box 2211
Fairfield, IA 52556
www.1stworldlibrary.org
First Edition

LCCN: 2006905707

Softcover ISBN: 1-4218-2136-2
Hardcover ISBN: 1-4218-2036-6
eBook ISBN: 1-4218-2236-9

Purchase *"Frank on a Gun-Boat"*
as a traditional bound book at:
www.1stWorldLibrary.org/purchase.asp?ISBN=1-4218-2136-2

1st World Library Literary Society is a nonprofit
organization dedicated to promoting literacy by:

- Creating a free internet library accessible from any computer worldwide.
- Hosting writing competitions and offering book publishing scholarships.

Readers interested in supporting literacy
through sponsorship, donations or
membership please contact:
literacy@1stworldlibrary.org
Check us out at: www.1stworldlibrary.ORG
and start downloading free ebooks today.

**Frank on a Gun-Boat**
*contributed by Tim, Ed & Rodney*
*in support of*
*1st World Library Literary Society*

# CONTENTS

# CHAPTER I

## IN THE NAVY

"Well, Frank, did you bring home the evening's paper?" inquired Mrs. Nelson, as her son entered the room where she was sitting.

"Yes, ma'am. Here it is!" answered Frank, producing it. "But there is no news in it. The Army of the Potomac has not moved yet. I don't see what makes them wait so long. Why don't McClellan go to work and thrash the rebels?"

"You must remember that the rebels have about as many men as we have," answered his mother. "Perhaps, if McClellan should undertake to 'thrash' the rebels, as you say, he would get whipped himself."

"That makes no difference," answered Frank. "If I was in his place, and the rebels *should* whip me, it wouldn't do any good, for I'd renew the battle every day, as long as I had a man left."

It was toward the close of the first year of the war, during the "masterly inactivity" of the Army of the Potomac. For almost eight months McClellan had been lying idle in his encampment, holding in check that splendid army, which, with one blow, could have crushed out the rebellion, and allowing the rebels ample time to encircle their capital with fortifications, before which the blood of loyal men was to be poured out like water. The people of the North were growing impatient; and

"On to Richmond!" was the cry from every part of the land.

From the time Fort Sumter had fallen, Frank had been deeply interested in what as going on. The insults which had been heaped upon the flag under which his grandfather had fought and died, made the blood boil in his veins, and he often wished that he could enlist with the brave defenders of his country. He grew more excited each day, as the struggle went on, and the news of a triumph or defeat would fire his spirit, and he longed to be standing side by side with the soldiers of the Union, that he might share in their triumphs, or assist in retrieving their disasters.

He was left almost alone now, for many of the boys of his acquaintance had shouldered their muskets and gone off with the others; and that very day he had met Harry Butler, who had enlisted as a private, wearing the uniform of a lieutenant, which he had won by his bravery at Fort Donelson.

He had never said one word to his mother about enlisting, for he was an only son, and he dreaded to ask her permission. But that mother's quick eye easily read what was going on in her son's mind. She had Puritan blood in her veins; her ancestors had fought in the war of the Revolution, and she had resolved that, if Frank wished to go, she would give her full consent. A mother's heart alone can tell the struggle it had cost her to come to this determination.

"I've got a letter from Archie, also," said Frank.

His mother took it from his hand, and read as follows:

Portland, *March* 18, 1862.

Dear Cousin:

I am about to tell you something which you will call strange news. Father has at last given his consent to my going to war, provided you will go too. He says that if I go, I must have you with me, to take care of me, and keep me straight. I suppose he thinks I will never go if I am obliged to wait for you, for he says your mother will not consent to your going. You can ask her, any way. You know you always wanted to have a hand in putting down this rebellion.

If we go at all, I think the best plan is to enter the navy. It is a much better branch of the service than the army - the discipline is better; there are no long marches to endure; and, wherever you go, your house goes with you.

Now, be sure and do your best, for now is our chance, if ever. Please write immediately, for I am afraid father will change his mind.

Yours, in haste, Archibald Winters.

When Mrs. Nelson had read the letter, she handed it back to her son without saying a word.

"Well, mother, what do you think of it?" inquired Frank.

"The matter rests entirely with you, my son," answered Mrs. Nelson, dropping her sewing into her lap. "Do just as you think best."

"Do you say I may go?" inquired Frank, joyfully.

"Certainly. You have my full consent to go, if you wish to."

"Oh, mother," exclaimed Frank, springing up and throwing his arms around her neck, "I wish I had known, long ago, that you were willing to have me go."

"Where are you going, Frank?" inquired Julia, who had a vague suspicion of what was going on.

"I 'm off to the war," answered her brother. "I am going into the navy with Archie."

"Oh, Frank," she exclaimed, bursting into tears, "you must not go. There's enough in the army without you. You will certainly get shot."

"I'll never be shot in the back," said Frank; "you may rely on that. But you don't suppose that every one who goes to war gets shot, do you? I may be one of the lucky ones; so don't cry any more."

But Julia could not control her feelings. The thought that her brother was to be exposed to the slightest danger was terrible; and Frank, seeing that it would do no good to talk to her, left the room, and went into his study, where he wrote to Archie, stating that he would start for Portland the next day. He spent the forenoon in wandering about the house and orchard, taking a long and lingering look at each familiar object. He locked the museum, and gave the key to Julia, who was close at his side wherever he went. Even Brave seemed to have an idea of what was going on, for he followed his master about, and would look into his face and whine, as though he was well aware that they were about to be separated.

Immediately after dinner, the carriage which was to convey Frank and his baggage to the Julia Burton drew up before the door. The parting time had come. "Good-by, mother," said Frank, as he stood at the door, ready to go.

"Good-by, my son," said Mrs. Nelson, straining him to her bosom, and struggling hard to keep back a sob. "We may never see you again, but I hope I shall never hear that you shrunk from your duty."

Frank could not reply - his breast was too full for utterance: and hastily kissing his sister, and shaking Hannah's hand, he hurried down the walk toward the gate. He had not gone far before Brave came bounding after him.

Harry Castlemon

"Go back, old fellow," said Frank, caressing the faithful animal; "you can't go with me this time. It will be a long while before you and I will go anywhere together again. Go back, sir."

Brave understood his master perfectly; and he turned and trotted toward the house, looking back now and then, and whining, as if urging his master to allow him to go too. Frank did not stop to look back, but sprang into the carriage, and the driver closed the door after him, and mounted to his seat and drove off. He had scarcely time to get his baggage on board the steamer before she moved off into the stream. And Frank was glad it was so, for the longer he remained in sight of the village, the harder grew the struggle to leave it. But, at length, every familiar object was left behind, and being surrounded by new scenes, Frank gradually recovered his usual spirits.

In two days he arrived at Portland, and as he was getting off the cars, he was seized by Archie, who had come to the depot to meet him.

"I'm glad to see you," said the latter; "it is lucky that you wrote just as you did, for father has said a dozen times that I can't go. But I guess he will not refuse me, now that you are here."

"I hope not," said Frank; "we can go as well as any one else. If every one was to stay at home, we shouldn't have any army at all."

"That's just what I told father; but he didn't seem to see it. He says there are some who ought to go, for they are of no earthly use here; but he thinks that boys like you and me ought to stay at home until we know enough to take care of ourselves."

But Mr. Winters did not raise many objections when he found that Frank had obtained his mother's consent; and, on the next day but one after Frank's arrival, he accompanied the boys on board the receiving-ship, where they were speedily examined and sworn in. Each was then supplied with a bag and hammock, and two suits of clothes; and, when they were rigged out in their blue shirts and wide pants, they made fine-looking sailors. At Mr. Winters' request they were granted permission to remain on shore until a raft of men was ready to be sent away. The boys were allowed to do pretty much as they pleased while they remained, for, as they were to leave so soon, Mr. Winters could not find it in his heart to raise any objections to the plans they proposed for their amusement. Besides, he knew that Archie was in good hands, for Frank was a boy of excellent habits, and possessed sufficient moral courage to say *no*, when tempted to do wrong; and, as he had great influence over his cousin, Mr. Winters knew their conduct would be such as he could approve.

At length, one morning, when they went on board the receiving-ship to report as usual, they were ordered to present themselves at the depot at two o'clock that afternoon, with their bags and hammocks, in readiness to take the train for the West. The boys were a good deal disappointed when they heard this, for the idea of serving out their year on the Mississippi River was not an agreeable one. They had hoped to be ordered to the coast. But, as Archie remarked, it was "too late to back out," and they were obliged to submit. When Archie came to bid farewell to his parents, he found it to be a much more difficult task than he had expected. The tears would come to his eyes, in spite of himself, as he embraced his mother; and, as soon as he could disengage himself from her arms, he seized his bag and hammock, and rushed out of the house to conceal his emotion. When they reached the depot, they found that the draft to which they belonged numbered nearly two hundred men, some of whom were old sailors, while others, like themselves, were entirely unacquainted with the life they were about to lead.

The journey to Cairo - which was then the naval depot of the Western rivers - was a long and tedious one. They were treated with the greatest kindness by the officers who accompanied them, and at almost every station the people would flock around the cars with baskets of provisions, which were freely distributed.

Early on the fifth morning they reached their destination, and were immediately marched on board a small steamer which lay alongside of the naval wharf-boat, and carried to the receiving-ship, which lay anchored in the middle of the river.

# CHAPTER II

## LEARNING THE ROPES

As they came on board the receiving-ship they were all drawn up in a line, the roll was called, and they were divided off into messes. The mess to which Frank and his cousin belonged was called "Number Twenty-five." As they were about to be dismissed, the officer who had called the roll said to Archie:

"You will be cook of this mess."

"Sir?" said Archie, in surprise.

"You will be cook of this mess," repeated the officer, in a louder tone. "But what is the matter with you? Are you hard of hearing?"

"No, sir; but I can't cook."

"Never mind; you can try. You may go below, lads."

The men did as they were ordered, and our heroes seated themselves on one of the broadside guns, and Archie said:

"I'm in a nice fix, ain't I? I don't know any more about cooking than a hog does about gunpowder."

"I will assist you all I can," said Frank; "but I wonder what we shall have for dinner? I hope it will be something good, for I'm

Harry Castlemon

as hungry as a bear."

At this moment the whistle of the boatswain's mate sounded through the ship, and that personage passed them and called out, in a low voice:

"Mess cook Number Twenty-five!"

"He means me, don't he?" inquired Archie, turning to his cousin.

"I don't know, I'm sure. Ask him."

"Mess cook Number Twenty-five," again shouted the mate.

"Here I am," said Archie.

"Well, you ought to be somewhere else," said the mate, sharply. "Why don't you go and draw your rations?"

"I don't know where I should go," answered Archie.

"Then fly around and find out;" and the mate turned on his heel and walked away.

"Now, that's provoking," exclaimed Archie. "Why couldn't he tell a fellow where to go? I'll tell that officer that I didn't ship for a cook; I shipped to fight. I wish I was at home again."

But regrets were worse than useless, and Archie began to look around to find some one who could tell him where to go to draw his rations. At length he met one of the men who belonged to his mess, whose name was Simpson, who told him that he must go to the paymaster's store-room, and offered to show him the way; and, as he saw that Archie was entirely unacquainted with life on shipboard, Simpson told him to come to him whenever he wanted any advice.

As Archie entered the store-room, the paymaster's steward, a boy about his own age, who was serving out the provisions, after inquiring the number of his mess, said:

"It's lucky that you came in just as you did, for I have sent the master-at-arms after you. If you don't attend to your business better than this, I shall have you put on the black-list for a week or two."

Now, Archie had never been accustomed to being "ordered about by any boy of his size," as he afterward remarked, and he felt very much like making an angry reply. But he knew it would only get him into trouble, and, choking down his wrath, he answered:

"If any one will tell me what my duty is, I shall be glad to do it."

"You haven't been in the navy a great while, have you?" inquired the steward, with a laugh.

"No; this is my first attempt at learning to be a sailor."

"Well, all I have got to say," continued the steward, "is, that you will soon be sorry that you ever made the attempt."

"I am sorry now," said Archie; "and if I ever get home again, you'll never catch me in another scrape like this. I don't like the idea of having everybody order me around, and talk to me as though I was a dog."

"No reflections," said the steward sharply. "Better keep a civil tongue in your head. But now to business. In the first place, here are your dishes," and he handed Archie a number of tin pots and plates, a large pan, and a mess-kettle.

"What shall I do with these?" asked Archie.

"Why, eat out of them, to be sure," answered the steward; "what else would you do with them? I shall hold you responsible for them," he continued; "and if any of them are lost, they will be charged to your account. Now go and put them away in your mess-chest, which you will find on the berth-deck, and then come back, and I will give you your rations."

Archie accordingly picked up his dishes, and started - he knew not whither, for he had no idea to which part of the vessel he should go in order to find the berth-deck. But he had often boasted that he would have no difficulty in getting along in the world while he had a tongue in his head; so he made inquiries of the first man he met, who told him to go up to the captain, who was always ready to send the executive officer to show landlubbers over the ship. If there was any joke in this, Archie was too angry to notice it, and he was about to make a suitable rejoinder, when a voice close behind him said:

"Now, shipmate, what's the use of being so hard on the boy?"

Archie turned, and found Simpson at his side.

"The youngster hain't been to sea as long as you and I have," continued the latter. "If we were ashore, he would stand a better chance of gettin' along than you nor me."

"Then, shiver his tim'ers, why didn't he stay ashore, where he belongs?" asked the man, gruffly.

"Oh, he's got the right stuff in him, and will soon learn the ropes," answered Simpson. "Come, now, my little marlin-spike," he continued, turning to Archie, "follow in my wake, and I'll show you where our mess-chest is;" and the kind-hearted sailor led the way to the berth-deck, and showed Archie the mess-chest, which had "No. 25" painted on it. Archie put all his dishes into it, with the exception of the mess-kettle and two plates, which, according to Simpson's directions, he took back to the store-room, to put his rations in. The steward then gave him a large piece of salt beef, some coffee, sugar, butter, and sea-biscuit.

"Is this all we have to eat?" inquired Archie, as he picked up his rations and followed Simpson back to his mess-chest.

"All!" repeated Simpson; "yes, my hearty, and you may thank your lucky stars that you have got even this. You'll have to live on worse grub nor this afore your year is out. But I see you don't like the berth of cook, so I'll take it off your hands. Give me the key of the chist."

Archie accordingly handed it over, and then went in search of his cousin, whom he found perched upon a coil of rope, engaged in writing a letter.

"Well," exclaimed the latter, as Archie came up, "how do you get along?"

"I don't get along at all," said Archie; "I tell you, we've got ourselves in a fix. What do you suppose we are going to have for dinner?"

"I don't know," answered Frank. "Well, we will have a chunk of salt beef, coffee without any milk, butter strong enough to go alone, and crackers so hard that you couldn't break them with an ax. I tell you, the navy is played out."

"Well, it can't be helped," said his cousin. "We are in for it. But we'll soon get accustomed to the food; we are seeing the worst of our year now."

"I certainly hope so," said Archie; "but I know I can stand it if any one else can; and when I fairly get started, I won't ask favors of any one."

Frank made no reply, but went on with his letter, and Archie leaned on one of the guns and gazed listlessly into the water. At length they were interrupted by the boatswain's whistle, blown three times in succession, long and loud.

"What's the matter now, I wonder," said Frank, as the sailors commenced running about the ship in all directions.

"I know," answered Archie, as he saw Simpson dive into the cook's galley and reappear bearing the mess-kettle, filled with steaming coffee, in one hand, and a large pan, containing the salt beef, in the other - "dinner is ready."

The cousins walked aft to their mess-chest, and found the berth-deck filled with men, who were sitting around the chests, brandishing their sheath-knives over plates fall of salt beef and "hard-tack."

Coming directly from home, where they had been accustomed to luxurious living, our young sailors thought they could not relish this hard fare but, as they had eaten no breakfast, they were very hungry, and the food tasted much better than they had expected.

When dinner was ended, Simpson began to gather up the dishes belonging to his mess, preparatory in washing them. Frank and Archie offered their assistance, and Simpson directed the former to take the mess-kettle and go up to the galley after some hot water. When he was returning, he saw a man stealing around the deck, holding something behind him that looked very much like a bundle of rope, and keeping a close watch on every one he met. Frank did not know what to make of this, and stepping up to the boatswain's mate, he inquired:

"What is that man doing with that bundle of rope behind him?"

"That ain't a bundle of rope, you landlubber," replied the mate; "that's a swab."

"Well, what is he doing with it?"

"The best way for you to learn would be for you to spill some of that water you have got in your kettle on the deck."

Frank, without stopping to think, tipped up his kettle, and turned out some of the water; and the man, who had been watching his every movement, sprang toward him and threw down the swab, exclaiming, "I've caught you, my hearty; now you may log this bit of rope for awhile."

"What do you mean?" inquired Frank, amid a roar of laughter from every sailor who had witnessed the performance. "What does he mean?" repeated the mate; "why, he means that you have got to wipe up that water you have spilt on deck, and carry that swab until you can catch some one else doing the same thing."

For the benefit of the uninitiated, we will make an explanation. It often happens on shipboard, especially receiving-ships, that the men become very careless; and in carrying water, paint, or grease about the ship, frequently spill some of it on deck. While this state of things continues, it is impossible to keep a ship clean, and, in order to break up this habit, the culprits are obliged to wipe up whatever they have spilled, and then carry a swab about the deck until they can detect some one else equally unfortunate. This is not a pleasant task; for, as soon as this rule is put in force, the men become very careful, and the luckless offender is sometimes obliged to walk the decks the entire day before he can detect any one in the act of violating it.

Frank, of course, did not understand this, and the mate had got him into the scrape for the purpose of getting the man who first had the swab, who was a particular friend of his, out of his unpleasant position.

"Come, youngster, drop that mess-kettle and pick up that swab," commanded the mate.

Frank knew he had no alternative; so he set his mess-kettle on deck out of the way, and picking up the swab, walked aft to the place where he had left Simpson.

"Hullo, there," exclaimed the latter, as Frank approached, "what's the matter with you?"

Frank related the whole circumstance, and Simpson could scarcely restrain his indignation.

"That bo'son's mate ought to be mast-headed for a whole week," he exclaimed. "But I'll square yards with him some day. I'm sorry you have got into this scrape, but it can't be helped. I've seen many a good fellow, in my time, in the same fix. Now you must walk around the ship, and if you see any one spill the least drop of water, or any thing else, on deck, rush up and give him the swab. There are a good many landlubbers on board, who don't know the rules, and you won't have any trouble in catching them. Always be careful to keep the swab behind you, out of sight."

Frank was a good deal mortified at being the victim of this novel mode of punishment; but he consoled himself with the thought that he would soon learn his duty, and be enabled to avoid all such scrapes. He walked about the vessel for an hour, trailing the swab along the deck behind him; but it seemed as though every one was particularly careful.

Meanwhile Archie, who had learned the particulars of the case from Simpson, was acting as a sort of scout, hoping to be of some assistance to his cousin. But he looked and waited in vain for some one to violate the rule, and finally he resolved to make use of a little strategy in releasing Frank.

Discovering a man coming out of the galley with a pail of water, Archie walked rapidly down the deck, and jostled him with sufficient force to empty half the contents of his pail on the deck. Archie did not, of course, stop to apologize, but hurried on, and before the man could look up to see who had caused the mischief, he had disappeared Frank, who had been watching his cousin's motions, immediately stepped up and dropped the swab before the man, and walked away, laughing in his sleeve, when he thought how cleverly his release had been accomplished.

When the hour of bedtime arrived, the boys were instructed how to get into their hammocks, and laughed at for tumbling out on the opposite side. But, after a few attempts, they succeeded in gaining the center of their suspended beds, and were soon in a sound sleep.

# CHAPTER III

## SQUARING THE YARDS

By degrees the boys became accustomed to their new situation, and began to feel much more contented. The only thing that troubled them was the food they received. It consisted, for the most part, of salt pork and beef, and hard crackers, with now and then a little flour and dried apples. Simpson, who had been in the navy nearly all his life, and had become well acquainted with its rules and regulations, asserted that they did not receive half their allowance, and promised that, if he could detect the paymaster's steward in the act of cheating them, he would pay him back in his own coin. Now Blinks, for that was the steward's name, was a notorious cheat; he never gave the men their full rations. On the contrary, he often boasted that he cleared not less than a hundred pounds of provisions every day. He was the caterer of the steerage mess, and many a pound of flour and apples, which should have been given to the men, found its way to his table, in the shape of pies and puddings. Blinks always rose early, and as soon as he was dressed, the steerage steward, every morning, brought to his room a lunch, consisting of coffee and apple-pie. He was very fond of pies, and had several made every day. Every time the men passed the galley, they saw long rows of them set out to cool. Many a midnight plundering expedition had been planned against the galley, but without success. The door and windows were securely fastened at sundown, and all attempts to effect an entrance were unavailing. It was also useless to attempt to bribe the cook, for Blinks, who was a strict accountant, always knew how many pies were made every day, and if any of them were missing, the cook was sure to suffer. One evening, while Frank and Simpson were engaged in washing up the supper-dishes, the latter inquired:

"Would you like one of those pies we saw in the galley to-day?"

"Yes," answered Frank; "they looked very tempting."

"Well," said Simpson, lowering his voice to a whisper, "we'll have some of them to-night."

"How will we get them?" inquired Frank.

"Why, we'll steal them. We can't beg or buy them. Besides, the stuff they are made of rightfully belongs to us. I don't care a snap for the pies, but I don't want to see that rascally steward growing fat off our grub."

"I'm in for it," answered Frank, who had long wanted an opportunity to revenge himself on Blinks.

"Will that cousin of yours lend us a hand?" inquired Simpson.

"Yes, without any coaxing. He does not like the steward any better than I do. But I'd like to know how we are going to work to get at the pies? The doors and windows are all fastened."

"We will pry up the galley, so that one of us can crawl under it. I've put a handspike where I can find it in a moment. We shall have no trouble at all."

As soon as the dishes were washed and stowed away in the mess-chest, Frank went to find his cousin, who was always ready for any mischief of that kind, and readily agreed to the proposal. When bedtime came, the three slung their ham-mocks together, and, to all appearances, were soon fast asleep.

At nine o'clock the ship's corporal put out all the berth-deck lights, which left the place shrouded in darkness. As soon as he had gone forward again, Simpson raised himself on his elbow, and whispered:

"Turn out, lads. Now's our time."

The boys crept noiselessly out of their hammocks, and followed the sailor, who led the way directly to the galley, which was, in fact, a small house, about ten feet square, built on the deck, to which it was insecurely fastened. Simpson found his handspike without any difficulty, and placing one end of it under the galley, easily raised it from the deck, while Archie threw himself on his hands and knees, and crawled in under it. It was as dark as pitch inside the galley, but he knew exactly where the pies were kept, and had no difficulty in finding them. He handed three of them to his cousin, and then crawled out again, and the galley was lowered to its place. After stowing the pies safely away in their mess-chest, they again sought their hammocks. The next morning, when the steward entered the galley to prepare the usual lunch for Blinks, he was surprised, and a good deal terrified, to find that some of the pies were missing. He immediately went on deck, and reported it to Blinks, who furiously asked:

"Where have they gone to, you rascal?"

"I don't know, sir, I'm sure," answered the steward, while visions of double-irons danced before his eyes. "There were eight pies in the galley when I locked it up last night."

"I don't believe it, you scoundrel. You sold the pies, and think that, by telling me they are missing, you can make me believe that they were stolen."

"I have never done any thing of the kind since I have been your steward, Mr. Blinks," said the man, with some spirit. "I have always been as careful of your interests as I would be of my own. Did you ever detect me in a mean or a dishonest act?"

"No; but I have often caught the cook stealing things. I'll report you to the executive officer, and have you punished. Go below."

The man sullenly withdrew, and Blinks hurried to the executive officer's room and reported the affair.

"Are you sure the steward stole the pies, Mr. Blinks?" inquired the officer; "perhaps some one broke into the galley. It would be well for you to go down and see, before punishing the steward."

Blinks hurried below, and commenced a thorough examination of the locks and window-fastenings, but all to no purpose; and he was still more surprised when the steward affirmed that he had found all the doors and windows closed, just as he had left them. This was also reported to the executive officer, who advised Blinks to say nothing about the affair, but to set a watch over the galley, and, if possible, discover the offender.

Blinks resolved to act upon this suggestion; and, the following evening, he posted a sentry over lite galley, with instructions to arrest any one who might be discovered prowling around. After fastening the doors and windows himself, he put the keys in his pocket and walked away.

At half-past nine o'clock our young sailors and Simpson were again on hand. After a careful reconnoissance, the sentry was discovered fast asleep at his post. They immediately set to work as before - the galley was raised up, and three more pies secured. It was all done in a moment, and the sentinel was not awakened; and as they retreated to their hammocks, they could scarcely refrain from laughing outright, when they thought how nicely the trick was performed.

The next morning Blinks opened the galley at an early hour, and was surprised and enraged to find that some of his pies were again missing. He carefully examined every nook and corner of the galley, but failed to discover a place where any one could effect an entrance.

For four nights more, in succession, Frank and his accomplices visited the galley, each time taking pies enough to last them a whole day; and Blinks, in the mean time, was making unavailing efforts to discover the offenders. On the fifth night, Archie, who was the one that always went into the galley, was much longer than usual in finding the pies. At length he whispered,

"I say, Simpson!"

"Ay, ay, my hearty; what is it?"

"I can't find but one pie."

"You can't, hey?" said Simpson; "I smell a rat. Bring the pie out here."

Archie accordingly handed it out, saying, as he did so -

"I'm hungry as blazes; I believe I'll eat a piece of that pie to-night."

"Not in a hurry," said Simpson, as they began to crawl back toward their hammocks; "not in a hurry; I've been in such scrapes as this before, and can't be fooled easy."

"What do you mean?" inquired Frank.

"Why, I mean that this pie was made on purpose for us," said Simpson; "it has got some kind of medicine in it that will make a fellow sick. If we should eat it, they would not be long in finding out who stole the pies."

"I'll tell you what to do with it," said Frank, suddenly; "let's give it to Jenkins, the boatswain's mate; he's a mean fellow, and I shouldn't be sorry to see him sick.'

"That's just what I was going to do with it," said Simpson. "Now, you go back to your hammocks, and I'll carry him the pie."

"As Simpson had taken particular notice of the place where Jenkins was in the habit of slinging his hammock, he had no difficulty whatever in finding it.

"I say, shipmate," he whispered, shaking the mate by the shoulder.

"What do you want?" he growled.

"Wake up," said Simpson; "I've got a nice pie for you; do you want it?"

"Of course I do," answered the mate, taking it from Simpson's hand. "But who are you?" he inquired, for it was so dark that he could not have recognized the features of his most intimate friend.

"I'm Jack Smith," answered Simpson; "but I can't stop to talk with you, for some one may discover me;" and before Jenkins could detain him, he had slipped off quietly in the darkness.

It was as Simpson had said - the pie had made "on purpose for them." When Blinks saw that it was impossible to discover the guilty party, he ordered his steward to make a nice large pie, into which he put two doses of jalap. It was his intention to make the offender sick; and he told the doctor what he had done, and requested him to keep an eye on all who came to him for medicine.

The next morning Jenkins was not heard blowing his whistle, but was seen moving slowly about the ship, with a pale, woe-begone countenance; and as soon as the doctor appeared, he made application to go on the "sick-list."

"What's the matter with you?" inquired the doctor.

Jenkins then explained how he had been suddenly taken very ill during the night, and was afraid he was going to die. The doctor, who knew in a moment that it was the effect of the medicine contained in the pie, exclaimed:

"Why, you're just the man Mr. Blinks has been wanting to see for the last week. Orderly, ask Mr. Blinks if he will have the kindness to come here a moment."

The orderly disappeared, and Jenkins stood, looking the very picture of despair, too sick to know or care what was going on.

"Mr. Blinks, I've found your man," said the doctor, when the paymaster's steward made his appearance.

"Well, my fine fellow," said Blinks, turning to the mate, and smiling grimly, "how do you feel by this time? Very pleasant morning, isn't it! I knew I'd catch you, you scoundrel," he exclaimed, suddenly changing his tune; "I'll teach you to steal my pies!"

"I - I - don't know what you mean, sir!" said the mate, in surprise.

"Don't talk to me, you villain," said Blinks savagely; "didn't you eat a pie last night?"

"Yes, sir," answered Jenkins, hesitatingly, "but" -

"I knew you did, you rascal."

"But the pie was given to me, sir," said the mate.

"Oh, that story won't do at all. I'll fix you. Go below."

In a short, time the mate, who was so weak that he was scarcely able to stand alone, was summoned before the captain, who gave him a severe reprimand, and disrated him. He came down on deck, looking very forlorn indeed; and as he passed by

Simpson, who, with Frank and Archie, was standing in the starboard gangway, the former exclaimed:

"That's what I call squaring the yards; I'm even with him now."

As soon as Jenkins had recovered from the effects of the physic, he began to make efforts to find Jack Smith. One day he approached Simpson who was seated on a coil of rope, spinning one of his forecastle yarns to Frank and Archie, and said:

"Shipmate, do you know any one aboard here named Jack Smith?"

"No," answered Simpson, with the utmost gravity, "I don't know any one who goes by that name."

"Well, there *is* a chap here by that name," said Jenkins, "and I wish I could find him. He got me into a bad scrape."

But, it is needless to say, he never found Jack Smith.

# CHAPTER IV

## A MIDNIGHT ALARM

On the afternoon of the following day, as Frank and his cousin were walking up and down the deck, talking over old times, Simpson hurriedly approached them, exclaiming,

"Boys, do you want to leave this ship?"

"Yes," answered Frank; "we're tired of staying here."

"Well, it's all right, then. I volunteered to go, and I had both your names put down. The executive officer says if you want to go, just get your donnage and go for'ard."

"Where are we to go?" inquired Archie.

"On board of the Illinois," answered Simpson. "She is a magazine-ship, and is lying half-way between here and Mound City. No work at all to do, I'm going.'

"Then we'll go, of course," said Frank; "for we don't want to lose you."

They immediately got down their hammocks and bags, and went forward, where they found the executive officer standing on the forecastle, waiting for them.

"Well, lads, do you volunteer to go on the Illinois?" he asked.

"Yes, sir."

"Jump down into that dingy, then," said the officer, pointing to a small boat that lay alongside.

The boys did as they were ordered, and just as they had finished storing away their bags and hammocks under the thwarts, a man dressed in the uniform of a sailor sprang down into the boat, exclaiming:

"Man your oars, lads, and shove off - you've a long pull before you."

Archie took one of the oars, Frank the other; Simpson stowed himself away in the bow of the boat, and the sailor took his seat at the helm.

The cousins were both good oarsmen, and they made the little boat dance over the water like a duck. It was full five miles to the place where the Illinois lay, and they soon found that it was indeed "a long, hard pull." The current was very strong, and it reminded the boys of many a tough struggle they had had around the head of Strawberry Island, in the Kennebec River.

In about two hours they reached the Illinois, and, as they sprang on board, their baggage was seized by willing hands, and carried to the cabin, which had been stripped of nearly all its furniture, and presented, altogether, a desolate appearance. After a few moments' conversation with one of their new messmates, they learned that there were only fifteen men on board the vessel, including one sergeant and two corporals. These were the only officers; and they were, in fact, no officers at all, for they were all rated, on the books of the receiving-ship, as "landsmen."

They soon discovered that there was no discipline among the crew - there could not be under the circumstances. Each stood a two-hour watch, at night, and assisted in pumping out the ship, morning and evening. With the exception of these duties, there was no work to be done on board the vessel. The remainder of the day was spent as suited them best. Some passed the time in hunting and nailing, some in reading, and some lounged about the decks, from morning until night.

Frank and Archie were very much pleased with their new situation. There was no boatswain's mate to trouble them, and they were in no danger of rendering themselves liable to punishment for some unintentional offense.

After stowing away their bags and hammocks, they amused themselves in strolling about the boat, until a neat-looking little sailor stepped up, and informed them that supper was ready. They followed him into the cabin, and took their seats at the table, with the rest, and one of the sailors, who went by the name of Woods, exclaimed:

"Now, boys, pitch in, help yourselves, for if you don't, you won't be helped at all. Every one that comes here has to learn to take care of himself."

"You will not find us at all bashful," answered Frank, and he began helping himself most bountifully to every thing on the table.

It did not take them long to become acquainted, and the boys found that their new shipmates were much better educated than the majority of the sailors they had met. They were a good-natured, jovial set of fellows, and the meal-hour passed away quickly and pleasantly.

Immediately after supper the corporal ordered all hands below to pump out the ship. In a quarter of an hour this was accomplished, and as they were ascending to the boiler-deck. Woods remarked:

"I wish I was back in Wisconsin again for a little while."

"Are you tired of the navy?" inquired Frank.

"Oh, no!" answered Woods; "but I should like to see my friends again, and try my hand at quail-shooting."

"Are you fond of hunting?"

"Yes, indeed; I spend all my spare time in the woods, when I am at home."

This was the very man, of all others, that Frank would have chosen for a companion, and he informed Woods that he also was very fond of rural sports. They seated themselves on the boiler door railing, and each related some of his hunting and fishing adventures, and, finally, Woods proposed that they should go over the river into Kentucky, on the following morning, on a squirrel hunt. Frank, of course, readily agreed to this. He immediately started in search of his cousin and Simpson, and informed them of the proposed excursion. When he returned to the place where he had left Woods, he found him with a musket on his shoulder, and a cartridge-box buckled about his waist, pacing up and down the deck.

"I'm on watch, you see," he said, as Frank came up, "You will go on at midnight; so you had better go and turn in. If we go hunting to-morrow, we must start by four o'clock at least, for we have a good way to walk before we reach the hunting-ground. Good night." And Woods, settling his musket more firmly on his shoulder, continued his beat, while Frank sought his hammock.

About midnight he was awakened by a hand laid on his shoulder, when, starting up, he found one of the corporals standing beside his hammock holding a lantern in his hand.

"Is your name Nelson?" he inquired.

Frank answered in the affirmative, and the corporal continued:

"Roll out, then, for it is time for you to go on watch. But be careful when you come out, or you'll be shot."

"Shot!" exclaimed Frank. "Who'll shoot me? Are there any rebels around here?"

"Yes, plenty of them. There are some out on the bank now. I was walking with Woods, when I happened to look up, and saw two men, with their muskets pointed straight at us; but we got out ofthe way before they had time to shoot. Hurry up, now, but don't expose yourself," and the corporal hurried aft, hiding his lantern under his coat of the went.

What Frank's feelings were, we will not attempt to say. He was not a coward, for we once saw him alone in the forest, standing face to face with a wounded wild-cat, with no weapon in his hands but an ax; but fighting a wild-cat and a rebel sharp-shooter were two widely different things. He had never heard the whistle of a hostile bullet, nor had he ever seen a rebel; and it is not to be wondered at, if his feelings were not of the most enviable nature. But he was not one to shrink from his duty because it was dangerous; and he drew on his clothes as quickly as possible, and seizing a musket and cartridge-box that stood in a rack close by the cabin door, he hurried aft, where he found Woods concealed behind the port wheel-house, and the corporal behind a chicken-coop. They both held their guns in readiness, and were peering into the woods, as if trying to pierce the thick darkness that enshrouded them. The Illinois was tied up close to the bank, which, as the water in the river was low, was about thirty feet in hight; and as the moon was shining very brightly, a person hidden in the bushes could distinctly see every thing on deck.

"Keep close there," said Woods, as Frank came up. "The corporal says he saw some guerrillas on the bank."

Frank accordingly concealed himself behind a stanchion, and his hand trembled considerably as he cocked his musket and brought it to his shoulder. They remained in this position for nearly a quarter of an hour, when, suddenly, something stirred in the bushes.

"There they are," whispered the corporal, drawing himself entirely out of sight, behind the chicken-coop. "Look out, they'll shoot in a moment."

Frank kept a close watch on the bushes, and presently discovered a white object moving about among them.

"I see something, boys," he said; "but it don't look to me like a man."

"Yes, it is a man," exclaimed the corporal, excitedly. "Shoot him."

In obedience to the order, Frank raised his gun to his shoulder, and an ounce ball and a couple of buckshot went crashing through the bushes. The commotion increased for a moment, and then ceased, and something that sounded very much like a groan issued from the woods.

"By gracious, you hit one of them," exclaimed the corporal. "That was a good shot. We'll teach these rebs that it isn't healthy to go prowling about here at night."

Frank hastily reloaded his musket, and they waited, impatiently, for nearly an hour, for the other guerrilla to show himself, but the woods remained as silent as death.

"I guess that shot finished them," said the corporal; "so I will go and turn in. Keep a good look-out," he added, turning to Frank, "and don't expose yourself too much."

Woods and the corporal then went into the cabin, and Frank was left to himself. A feeling of loneliness he had never before experienced came over him. At first he determined to go and call his cousin to come and stand watch with him, so that he would have some one to talk with; but, on second thought, he remembered that Archie was to come on watch at two o'clock, and probably would not like to be disturbed. Besides, if he called him, it would look as though he was a coward, and afraid to stand his watch alone; so he gave up the idea, and remained in his place of concealment. Once he thought he discovered the sheen of a musket among the bushes; but it was only his imagination, and after waiting half an hour without hearing any thing suspicious, he shouldered his gun, and commenced pacing the deck, in full view of the woods. But he was not molested, and when two o'clock came he saw a figure steal cautiously out of the cabin, and creep along toward him, under cover of the wheel-house. As he approached nearer, Frank recognized his cousin.

"Where are the rebs?" inquired the latter.

"The corporal said he saw two of them out there in the woods," answered Frank, pointing to a thick clump of bushes that stood on the edge of the bank; "and there was *something* out there, and I shot at it. But I've been on deck here, in plain sight, for the last hour, and haven't seen any thing."

"I hope there are no rebs in there," said Archie; "but I'll keep dark for awhile. I shipped to fight, but I don't like the idea of having a fellow send a bullet into me when I can't see him," and he began to settle himself into a comfortable position behind the chicken-coop.

"I don't think there is any danger," said Frank; "but perhaps it is well to be careful at first. Be sure and call us when you come off watch," and he shouldered his rifle and walked leisurely into the cabin.

# CHAPTER V

## A DISCOMFITED REBEL

Archie stood his watch without seeing or hearing any thing of the rebels, and when he was relieved, at four o'clock, he aroused Simpson, Woods, and his cousin, and after they had tied up their hammocks, and stowed them away in the nettings, Woods went to the sergeant's room to obtain his consent to their proposed excursion. This was easily accomplished, and while they were filling their pockets with musket-cartridges, Frank proposed that they should go out and see what it was that had occasioned the alarm during the night; so they leaned their muskets up in one corner of the cabin, and ran out on the bank, and there, weltering in his blood, lay, not a rebel, but a white mule. He it was that, while feeding about in the woods, had occasioned the disturbance in the bushes, and Frank's shot had done its work. The two men with muskets had existence only in the corporal's imagination. Simpson burst into a loud laugh.

"A nice set of fellows you are," he exclaimed. "I shouldn't want you stationed at my gun in action."

"Why not?" inquired Frank.

"Why, because you can't tell the difference between a mule and a secesh."

Frank made no reply to this, for, although he was very much

Harry Castlemon

relieved to find that it was a mule, and not a man, that he had killed, he was a good deal mortified at first, for he expected to be made the laughing-stock of his companions. But he consoled himself with the thought that he was not to blame. The corporal had said that he had seen guerrillas in the woods, and he had, as in duty bound, done his best to drive them away; besides, he would not have fired his gun had he not been ordered to do so.

"It's no matter," said Simpson, who noticed that Frank looked a little crest-fallen; "It was the corporal's fault."

"I know it," said Frank. "But that's poor consolation. I killed the mule, and shall probably be laughed at for it."

"What's the odds?" asked Simpson. "I've seen many a better man than you laughed at. But let us be going, for we have a long way to walk."

They accordingly retraced their steps to the vessel, and Woods awoke one of the corporals, who had volunteered to row them over into Kentucky. The dingy, which was kept fastened to the stern of the Illinois, was hauled alongside, and, in a few moments, they reached the opposite shore. Our four hunters sprang out, and, bidding the corporal good-by, shouldered their muskets, and disappeared in the forest. Woods, who was well acquainted with the "lay of the land," led the way. Just at sunrise they reached a ridge covered with hickory and pecan-trees.

"Here we are," he exclaimed, as he leaned on his gun, and wiped his forehead with his coat-sleeve. "There are plenty of squirrels around here. But I'm hungry; we have plenty of time to eat some breakfast before we begin."

They seated themselves under the branches of some small hickories, and Simpson produced from a basket some salt pork, hard crackers, and a bottle of cold coffee. Their long walk had given them good appetites, and the meal, homely as it was, was eaten with a relish. After they had rested a few moments, they started off in different directions, to commence the hunt. As Frank walked slowly along, with his gun on his shoulder, he could not help thinking of the many times he had been on such excursions about his native village. What a change a year had made! The "Boys of Lawrence" were no longer amateur sportsmen. They were scattered all over the country, engaged in the work of sustaining the integrity of the best government on earth. Would they ever all meet again? It was not at all likely. Perhaps some had already been offered up on the altar of their country; and if he should ever live to return home, there would be some familiar faces missing. In short, Frank was homesick. Finding himself once more in his favorite element had made him think of old times. He wandered slowly along, recalling many a fishing frolic and boat-race he had engaged in, until a loud chatter above his head roused him from his reverie. He looked up just in time to see a large squirrel striving to hide himself among the leaves on a tree that stood close by. Frank's gun was at his shoulder in a moment, and taking a quick aim at the squirrel, he pulled the trigger. But the old Springfield musket was not intended for fine shooting; for, though the shot cut the leaves all around, the squirrel escaped unhurt, and, running up to the topmost branch, again concealed himself. While Frank was reloading, Archie came up, and stood leaning on his gun, with rather a dejected air. "What's the matter with you?" inquired Frank.

"I wish I was down to the river," answered Archie.

"What would you do there? go fishing?"

"No, but I'd sink this musket so deep that no one would ever find it again. It don't shoot worth a row of pins. If I was standing twenty feet from the side of a barn, I couldn't hit it, I wish I had my shot-gun here."

"So do I," answered Frank; "I would very soon bring down that squirrel. I'm going to try him again;" and going around to the side of the tree where the squirrel had taken refuge, he fired again, but with no better success. The squirrel, not in the least injured, appeared amid a shower of leaves, and speedily found a new hiding-place.

"It's no use, I tell you," said Archie; "you can't hit any thing with that musket."

"It does look a little that way. But I must have that squirrel, if I have to shoot all day. Haven't you got a load in your gun?"

"Yes; but I might as well have none. I can kill as many squirrels by throwing the musket at them, as I can by shooting at them."

"Never mind, fire away - the ammunition doesn't cost us any thing."

"I know it; but another thing, this musket kicks like blazes. I had as soon stand before it, as behind it. But I'll try him;" and Archie raised his gun and blazed away. This time there was no mistake; the squirrel was torn almost to pieces by the ball; and when the smoke cleared away, Frank saw his cousin sitting on the ground, holding both hands to his nose, which was bleeding profusely.

"You've killed the squirrel," he said.

"Yes," answered Archie; "but I hurt myself as much as I did him."

Frank was a good deal amused, and could scarcely refrain from laughing at his cousin's misfortune. He tried to keep on a sober face, but the corners of his mouth would draw themselves out into a smile, in spite of himself. Archie noticed this, and exclaimed:

"Oh, it's a good joke, no doubt."

"If you would hold your gun firmly against your shoulder,"

said Frank, "it wouldn't hurt half so bad. But hadn't we better go on?"

Archie raised himself slowly from the ground, and they moved off through the woods. The squirrels were very plenty; but it required two or three, and, sometimes, as many as half a dozen shots, to bring one down.

At length, after securing four squirrels, their shoulders became so lame that they could scarcely raise their guns; so they concluded to give up shooting, and start in search of Woods and Simpson, who had gone off together. About noon they found them, sitting on the fence that ran between the woods and a road. Simpson had three squirrels in his hand.

"We are waiting for you," he said, as Frank and Archie came up; "it's about time to start for the boat."

"I'm hungry," said Frank; "why can't we go down to that house and hire some one to cook our squirrels for us?"

"That's a good idea," said Woods; "come along;" and he sprang off the fence, and led the way toward the house spoken of by Frank, which stood about a quarter of a mile down the road, toward the river.

As they opened the gate that led into the yard, they noticed that a man, who sat on the porch in front of the house, regarded them with a savage scowl on his face.

"How cross that man looks!" said Archie, who, with his cousin, was a little in advance of the others; "maybe he's a reb."

"How do you do, sir?" inquired Frank, as he approached the place where the man was sitting.

"What do yees want here?" he growled, in reply.

"We came here to see if we couldn't hire some one to cook a

good dinner for us," answered Frank.

"No, ye can't," answered the man, gruffly; "get out o' here. I never did nothin' for a Yank, an' I never will. I'd like to see yer all drove from the country. Get out o' here, I tell yer," he shouted, seeing that the sailors did not move, "or I'll let my dogs loose on yer!"

"Why, I really believe he is a reb," said Archie; "he's the first one I ever saw. He looks just like any body else, don't he, boys?"

"If yees don't travel mighty sudden, I'll make a scatterin' among yer," said the man, between his clenched teeth; "I'll be dog-gone if I don't shoot some o' yer;" and he reached for a long double-barrel shot-gun that stood behind his chair.

"Avast, there, you old landlubber," exclaimed Simpson; "just drop that shootin' iron, will you. We're four to your one, and you don't suppose that we are going to stand still and be shot down, like turkeys on Thanksgivin' morning, do you? No, sir, that would be like the handle of a jug, all on one side. Shootin' is a game two can play at, you know. Come, put that we'pon down;" and Simpson held his musket in the hollow of his arm, and handled the lock in a very significant manner.

The man saw that the sailors were not to be intimidated, and not liking the way Simpson eyed him, he leaned his gun up in the corner again, and muttered something about Yankee mudsills and Abolitionists.

"Just clap a stopper on that jaw of yours, will you," said Simpson; "or, shiver my timbers, if we don't try man-o'-war punishment on you. Now, Frank," he continued, "you just jump up there, and shoot off the old rascal's gun; and then keep an eye on him, and don't let him get out of his chair; and the rest of us will look around and see what we can find in the way of grub."

Frank sprang up the steps that led on to the porch, and fired both barrels of the gun into the air, and then, drawing a chair to the other end of the porch, coolly seated himself, and deposited his feet on the railing; while the others went into the house, where they secured a pail of fresh milk and a loaf of bread. From the house they went into the wood-shed, where they found a quantity of sweet potatoes. They then returned to the place where they had left Frank.

"Come on, now," said Woods; "we'll have a tip-top dinner, in spite of the old secesh.

"Hold on," said Frank; "where are you going? I move we cook and eat our dinner here. There's a stove in the house, and every thing handy."

The man was accordingly invited into his own house by the boys, and requested to take a seat, and make himself perfectly at home, but to be careful and not go out of doors. They deposited their muskets in one corner of the room; and while Archie started a fire in the store, Frank dressed the squirrels, and washed some of the sweet potatoes, and placed them in the oven to bake. Woods drew the table out into the middle of the room; and Simpson, after a diligent search, found the cupboard, and commenced bringing out the dishes Frank superintended the cooking; and, in half an hour, a splendid dinner was smoking on the table. When the meal was finished, they shouldered their muskets, and Simpson said to the man:

"Now, sir, we're very much obliged to you for your kindness; but, before we go, we want to give you a bit of advice. If you ever see any more Yankee sailors out this way, don't try to bully them by talking treason to them. If you do, just as likely as not you'll get hold of some who won't treat you as well as we have. They might go to work and clean out your shanty. Good day, sir;" and Simpson led the way toward the boat.

# CHAPTER VI

## FRANK'S FIRST EXPLOIT

During the three months following that Frank and Archie were attached to the Illinois, they met with no adventure worthy of notice. They passed nearly every day in the woods, and, after considerable practice, had become splendid shots with their muskets; and as game was abundant, their table was kept well supplied.

At length, the new magazine-boat, which had for some time been building at Cairo, was towed alongside the Illinois, and a detachment of men from the receiving-ship were set to work to transfer the ammunition. The crew of the Illinois were not at all pleased with this, for they knew that the easy life they had been leading was soon to be brought to an end.

When the ammunition had all been removed into the new boat, the steamer Champion came alongside, and the Illinois was towed down to Columbus, where she was to undergo repairs, and her crew was transferred to the receiving-ship again.

The day after they arrived on board, while Frank and his cousin were seated on a coil of rope, as usual, talking over old times, and wondering how George and Harry Butler liked the army, and why they had not written, the boatswain's mate came along, and called out, in a loud voice:

"Archie Winters!"

"Here I am," said Archie.

"Well, go up on deck," said the mate; "the captain wants to see you."

"The captain wants to see me!" repeated Archie, in surprise.

"Yes; and you had better bear a hand, too, for the captain isn't the man to wait long when he sends after any one."

Archie accordingly went on deck, trying all the while to think what he had done that was wrong, and expecting a good blowing up for some unintentional offense. Perhaps the captain had by some means learned who it was that had made the descent on the cook's galley, and had called him up for the purpose of punishing him.

Finding the captain on deck, talking with the executive officer, he very politely remained out of hearing, holding his hat in his hand, and waited for a chance to speak to him. At length the captain inquired:

"Hasn't Winters come up yet?"

"Yes, sir," answered Archie, stepping up with his best salute.

"Is this your writing?" inquired the captain, holding out to Archie a letter addressed, in a splendid business hand, to James Winters, Esq., Boston.

"Yes, sir," answered Archie; "that's a letter I wrote to my father."

"Well," continued the captain, "I have got a splendid position for you, as second clerk in the fleet paymaster's office. Would you like to take it?"

"Yes, sir," answered Archie; "but - but" -

"But what?" inquired the captain.

"I don't like to be separated from my cousin. We shipped together, and I should like to remain with him as long as possible."

"Oh, as to that," said the captain, "you can't expect to be together long; there is no certainty that you will be ordered to the same ship. You might as well separate one time as another. I think you had better accept this position."

"I should like to speak with my cousin before I decide, sir."

"Very well; look alive, and don't keep me waiting."

Archie touched his hat, and hurried below.

"What did he want with you?" inquired Frank, who was sitting with Simpson on their mess-chest.

Archie told his story, and ended by saying:

"I don't believe I'll take it; for I don't want to leave you."

"You're foolish," said Simpson; for, as the captain said, you can't expect to remain together a great while. To-morrow one of you may be ordered to a vessel in the Cumberland River, and the other to the lower fleet. Better take it; Frank can take care of himself."

"Yes" said Frank, "I should certainly take it, if I were in your place. You'll be an officer then, you know."

"Yes, I shall be an officer," said Archie, contemptuously; "and if I meet one of you anywhere, I mustn't associate with you at all. No sir; I'll go and tell the captain I can't take it."

"But, hold on a minute," said Frank, as his cousin was about to move away; "perhaps you may find that there is another good place, and then you can recommend me."

"That's so," said Archie; "I did not think of that; I believe I'll take it;" and he hurried on deck again.

"Well, what conclusion have you come to?" inquired the captain. "Will you take it?"

"Yes, sir, with many thanks for your kindness."

"What is your cousin's name?"

Archie told him, and the captain continued:

"I'll keep an eye open for him. I don't forget that I was young once myself; and I know that a sailor's life is rather tough for one who is not accustomed to it; and when I find a deserving young man, I like to help him along. Mr. Tyler," he continued, turning to the officer of the deck; "please send this young man over to the fleet paymaster's office in the first boat that leaves the ship. You need not take your donnage," he said, turning to Archie again; "if you suit the paymaster, you can come over for it at any time."

"Very good, sir," answered Archie; and he went below again.

When the ten o'clock boat was called away, Archie, in obedience to the captain's order, was sent over to the paymaster's office; and Frank was left alone. He watched the boat until it reached the landing, and he saw his cousin spring out. He then walked aft, and seated himself on the mess-chest, and commenced writing a letter to his mother. While he was thus engaged, he heard the order passed, in a loud voice: "All you men that belonged to the Illinois, muster on the forecastle with your bags and hammocks."

As Frank hastened to obey the order, he met Simpson,

who exclaimed:

"We're off again, my hearty; and I'm glad of it. I don't like to lay around here."

"Where are we going?" inquired Frank.

"I don't know for certain; but I suspect we are to be the crew of the store-ship Milwaukee, now lying alongside the wharf-boat."

Simpson's surmise proved to be correct. The entire crew of the Illinois, with the exception of Archie, was mustered around the capstan; and after answering to their names, they were crowded into a cutter that lay alongside, and, in a few moments, were landed on board the Milwaukee.

She had steam up; her stores were on board, and she was all ready to sail; and the crew had scarcely time to stow away their bags and hammocks, when the order was passed: "All hands stand by to get ship under way."

The gang-planks were quickly hauled in; the line with which she was made fast to the wharf-boat was cast off, and the Milwaukee was soon steaming down the river, and Cairo was rapidly receding from view.

The Milwaukee, which was now dignified by the name of "store-ship," was an old river packet. She was loaded with clothing, provisions, and small stores, with which she was to supply the fleet. It was not, of course, intended that she should go into action; but, in order that she might be able to defend herself against the guerrillas, which infested the river between Cairo and Helena, she mounted a twelve-pound howitzer on her boiler-deck, and was well supplied with muskets. Her destination was Helena.

They reached that place without any adventure, and, after supplying the fleet with stores, started to return to Cairo. One pleasant afternoon, as they were passing through Cypress Bend, the officer of the deck discovered a man standing on the bank, waving a flag of truce. A bale of cotton lay near him; and the man, as soon as he found that he had attracted their attention, pointed to the cotton, and signified, by signs, that he wished it carried up the river.

The Milwaukee was immediately turned toward the shore, and as soon as they arrived within speaking distance, the captain called out:

"What do you want?"

"I would like to have you take this cotton to Cairo for me," answered the man.

"Are you a loyal citizen?" asked the captain.

"Yes, sir; and here is a permit from Admiral Porter to ship my cotton;" and, as the man spoke, he held up a letter to the view of the captain.

"Bring her into the bank, Mr. Smith," said the captain, addressing the pilot; "and, Mr. O'Brien," he continued, in a lower tone, turning to an officer who stood near, "go down and stand by that howitzer. Perhaps there is no treachery intended, but it is well to be on the safe side."

As soon as the Milwaukee touched the bank, Frank and Simpson, with two others, sprang ashore with a line, and, after making it fast to a tree, returned on board, and commenced pushing out a plank, so that the cotton could be easily rolled on, when, suddenly, several men rose from behind the levee, and the quick discharge of their rifles sent the bullets around those standing on the forecastle, like hailstones; and Simpson, who was standing directly in front of Frank, uttered a sharp cry of pain, and sank heavily to the deck. The next moment the guerrillas, with loud yells, sprang down the bank in a body, intending to board the boat and capture her. But they had not taken her so much by surprise as they had imagined, for a shell from the howitzer exploded in their very midst, and one of the rebels was killed, and three disabled. The others turned and hastily retreated behind the levee. Frank took advantage of this, and lifting the insensible form of his friend, retreated under cover, and laid him on a mattress behind a pile of coal, where he would be safe from the bullets of the guerrillas, which now began to come through the sides of the boat in every direction.

This was the first time Frank had ever been under fire, and he was thoroughly frightened; but he knew that it was his duty to resist the rebels, and to do them as much damage as possible; so, instead of looking round for a safe place to hide, his first impulse was to run up on deck after a gun. This he knew was a dangerous undertaking, for the vessel lay close to the bank, the top of which was on a level with the boiler-deck; and behind the levee, scarcely half a dozen rods distant, were the guerrillas, who were ready to shoot the first man that appeared.

Nevertheless, Frank resolved to make the attempt, for he wanted to take revenge on them for shooting Simpson. But, just as he was about to start out, he heard the captain shout down through the trumpet which ran from the pilot-house to the engine-room:

"Back her, strong! We must get away from the bank or they will pick us all off."

In obedience to the order, the engineers let on the steam, and a heavy puffing told Frank that the powerful engines were doing their utmost to break the line which held them to the bank. Here was another thing that Frank knew he ought to do; he knew that he ought to cut that line, for it would be an impossibility to break it. There was an ax handy, and a sudden rush and a couple of lusty strokes would put the vessel out of danger. But, at short intervals, he heard the bullets crashing through the side of the boat, and he knew that the guerrillas were on the watch. If he made the attempt he could scarcely hope to come back alive; and he thought of his mother and Julia, how badly they would feel when they heard of his death. But even where he stood he was in danger of being struck by the bullets that were every moment coming through the vessel; and would not his mother much rather hear that he fell while performing his duty, than that he was shot while standing idly by, taking no part in the fight? He did not wait to take a second thought, but seized the ax, and, with one bound, reached the gangway that led out on to the forecastle. Here he hesitated again, but it was only for a moment. Clutching his ax with a firmer hold, and gathering all his strength for the trial, he sprang forward, and a few rapid steps brought him to the capstan, to which the line was made fast. He raised his ax, and one swift blow severed the line, and the Milwaukee swung rapidly out from the bank Without waiting an instant, Frank turned and retreated; but, instead of going back to the place where he had left Simpson, he bounded up the steps that led to the boiler-deck, and the next moment was safe behind a pile of baled clothing. His sudden appearance had taken the rebels completely by surprise, and before they could recover themselves, the line had been cut, and the young hero was safe. But they had seen where he had taken refuge, and, with loud yells of disappointment and rage, sent their bullets about his hiding-place in a perfect shower. Frank, however, knowing that he was safe, was not in the least alarmed. Waiting until the fire slackened a little, he sprang up, and, snatching a musket and cartridge-box from the rack which stood close by the door of the cabin, was back to his hiding-place in a moment.

"Now," he soliloquized, "we are on more equal terms. Better keep close, or I'll drop some of you."

In his cool, sober moments, Frank would have shuddered at the thought of taking the life of a fellow-being; but he had seen Simpson shot down before his eyes - perhaps killed; and is it to be wondered that he wished to avenge his fall?

It was some time before Frank could get an  opportunity to use his musket; for if he exposed the smallest portion of his body, it was the signal for his watchful enemies, who sent the bullets about him in unpleasant proximity. In spite of his dangerous situation, he could not help thinking that the rebels were very proficient in "Indian fighting," for, with all his watchfulness, he could not get an opportunity to put in a shot. All he could see of his enemies would be, first, a rifle thrust carefully over the levee, then a very small portion of a head would appear, and the bullet would come straight to the mark.

In the mean time the Milwaukee was working her way out into the stream, and the rebels, finding that their fire was not returned, grew bolder by degrees, and became less careful to conceal themselves. This was what Frank wanted; but he reserved his fire until a tall rebel rose to his full hight from behind the levee, fired his gun, and stood watching the effect of the shot. Frank's musket was at his shoulder in an instant, his finger pressed the trigger, and the rebel staggered for a moment, and disappeared behind the levee.

"There," said Frank to himself, "that's what Simpson would call 'squaring the yards.' I'm even with the rascals now."

The rebels answered the shot with load yells, and their bullets fell thicker than ever; but the Milwaukee was almost out of range, and, in a few moments, the firing ceased altogether.

# CHAPTER VII

## ON A GUN-BOAT

When the Milwaukee was fairly out of range of the bullets of the guerrillas, Frank put his gun back in the rack, and started in search of the doctor's steward. He ran into the cabin without ceremony, and was about to enter the steward's room, when he discovered a pair of patent-leather boots, which he thought he recognized, sticking out from under a mattress which lay on the cabin floor; and, upon examination, he found that it concealed the steward, who was as pale as a sheet, and shaking as though he had been seized with the ague.

"What do you want here?" he asked, in a trembling voice, as Frank raised the mattress.

"Simpson is shot," answered Frank, "and I would like to have you come down and see him."

"Do you suppose I am fool enough to go out on deck, and run the risk of being shot? No, sir; I'll stay here, where I am safe;" and the steward made an effort to draw his head under the mattress again.

"There's no danger now," said Frank; "the rebels have stopped firing. Besides, we are out of" -

"Go away, and let me alone," whined the steward.

"I am not going to expose myself."

"You're a coward," exclaimed Frank, now fairly aroused "But I guess the captain can" -

"Oh, don't," entreated the steward; "I haven't been here a minute. I started to get a gun, to pay the rebels back in their own coin; but the bullets came through the cabin so thick that I thought it best to retreat to a safe place;" and the steward threw off the mattress, and arose, tremblingly, to his feet.

"You went after a gun, did you?" inquired Frank, in a tone of voice which showed that he did not believe the steward's story.

"Yes; and I would have given them fits, for I am a dead shot."

"Where did you put your gun when you found that you had to retreat?"

"I put it back in the rack again."

This was a likely story; for a person as badly frightened as was the steward would not have stopped to put the gun back in its place; and, in his heart, Frank despised the man who could be guilty of such a falsehood.

As they were about to go out on deck, the steward drew back, exclaiming:

"I don't hardly believe it is safe to go out there just yet. Let us wait a few moments."

"I shan't wait an instant," said Frank. "Simpson has been neglected too long already. You can come down and attend to him, or not, just as you please." So saying, he opened the cabin door, and walking rapidly out, descended the stairs that led to the main deck.

The steward dreaded to follow; but he knew that, if he did not attend the wounded sailor, he would be reported to the captain, who, although a kind-hearted man, was a strict disciplinarian, and one who always took particular pains to see that his crew was well provided for. He dared not hesitate long; so, drawing in a long breath, he ran swiftly out on deck, and disappeared down the stairs like a shot.

Frank found Simpson sitting upon the mattress where he had been lain, with his elbows on his knees, and his head supported by his hands. As Frank came up, he said, in a weak voice:

"I came very near losing the number of my mess, didn't I? The rascals shot pretty close to me;" and he showed Frank an ugly-looking wound in the back of his head, from which the blood was flowing profusely.

By this time the steward arrived. After examining the wound, he pronounced it very severe, and one that would require constant attention.

Simpson was speedily conveyed to the sick bay, and every thing possible done to make him comfortable. Although the Milwaukee was completely riddled by the bullets of the guerrillas, he was the only one hurt. Frank was excused from all duty, that he might act as Simpson's nurse; and he scarcely left him for a moment during the two weeks of fever and delirium that followed. By the time they reached Cairo, however, he was pronounced out of danger.

Frank wanted very much to see his cousin; but the Milwaukee was anchored out in the river, and no one was allowed to go ashore. One afternoon, as he sat by his friend's hammock, reading aloud a letter from Harry Butler, in which he gave a vivid description of a late battle in which his regiment had participated, the orderly entered and informed him that the captain wished to see him. He followed the orderly, and, as he entered the cabin, the captain said:

"Please help yourself to a chair, Mr. Nelson; I shall be at

liberty in a moment. I should like to finish this letter before the mail-steamer sails. You will excuse me, will you not?"

"Certainly, sir," answered Frank; and he seated himself, lost in wonder.

The captain had addressed him as *Mr.* Nelson, while heretofore he had always been called, by the officers, Nelson, or Frank. What could it mean? The captain had always treated him with the greatest kindness; but, since the engagement with the guerrillas, all the officers had shown him more consideration than ever. He had noticed the change, and wondered at it.

At length the captain, after hastily directing the letter he had written, and giving it in charge of the orderly, took an official document from his desk, saying, as he did so:

"I am greatly pleased, Mr. Nelson, to be able to give you this, for you deserve it;" and after unfolding the letter, he gave it to Frank, who read as follows:

NAVY DEPARTMENT, WASHINGTON, D.C., Dec. 18, 1862.

Sir: For your gallantry in the late action at Cypress Bend, on the 1st inst., you are hereby appointed an Acting Master's Mate in the Navy of the United States, on temporary service. Report, without delay, to Acting Rear-Admiral David D. Porter, for such duty as he may assign you. Very respectfully, your obedient servant,

GIDEON WELLES, *Secretary of the Navy,*

Acting Master's Mate FRANK NELSON,
*S.S. Milwaukee, Mississippi Squadron.*

"Well," said the captain, after Frank had read the letter over three times, to make sure that he was not dreaming, and that he was really an officer, "what do you think of it?"

"I hardly know what to think, sir," answered Frank. "It is an honor I did not expect."

"Very likely," said the captain, with a laugh; "but you deserve it. If it hadn't been for you, we should all have been captured. I saw the whole of the transaction from the pilot-house."

"It was my duty to do it, sir."

"It was a brave act, call it what else you will. Now go and give this to the paymaster," continued the captain, handing Frank an order for the settlement of his accounts, "and then go immediately and report to the Admiral."

Frank left the captain, a good deal elated at his success; and when he approached Simpson, the latter exclaimed:

"What is it, my hearty? Your promotion?"

"Yes," answered Frank; "read that;" and he handed his appointment to his friend, who said:

"I knew you would get it. The captain isn't the man to let such a thing as you did at Cypress Bend pass unnoticed. Give us your flipper, my boy; I'm glad to see you an officer." And the brave fellow actually shed tears, as he shook Frank's hand. "Now, when you are ordered to your ship," he continued, "I wish you would speak a word for me. I am very well contented here, but I had much rather sail with you."

Frank promised to do his best, and, after putting on his "shore togs," as Simpson called them, and giving the captain's order to the paymaster, he started off to report to the Admiral.

When he arrived on board the flag-ship, he was met by the officer of the deck, who inquired his business.

"I wish to see the Admiral, sir" answered Frank; "I am ordered to report to him."

The officer immediately led the way aft, and showed Frank a marine standing at the door of the cabin, who took his name and disappeared. In a moment he returned, and informed Frank that the Admiral was waiting to see him.

He entered the cabin, and handed his appointment to the Admiral, who, after reading it, said:

"So, you are the young man that saved the Milwaukee, are you? Take a chair, sir."

In a few moments his orders to report, without delay, on board the Ticonderoga, were ready; and as the Admiral handed them to him, he said:

"Now, young man, you will be on a ship where you will have a chance to distinguish yourself. I shall expect to hear a good account of you."

"I shall always endeavor to do my duty, sir," answered Frank; and he made his best bow and retired.

When he returned to the Milwaukee, his accounts had all been made out. After the paymaster paid him up in full, Frank started for the nearest clothing-store, and when he came out, he was changed into a fine-looking officer.

He immediately directed his steps toward the naval wharf-boat, where he found a lively little fellow, who seemed full of business, superintending the loading of a vessel with provisions. It was Archie Winters; but it was plain that he did not recognize his cousin in his new uniform, for Frank stood close behind him, several moments, and Archie even brushed against him, as he passed.

"Can you tell me, sir, where I can find Mr. Winters?" inquired

Frank, at length.

"Yes, sir," answered Archie, promptly, looking his cousin full in the face; "I'm the - why, Frank, how are you?" and he seized his cousin's hand, and shook it heartily. "I've been on board the Milwaukee twice this morning, but you were off somewhere. I heard you had a fight down the river, with the rebels. But what are you doing? What boat are you ordered to?"

"I am not doing any thing at present," answered Frank; "but I am ordered to report on board the Ticonderoga."

"There she is," said Archie, pointing to a long, low, black vessel that lay alongside of the wharf boat. "I am just putting provisions on board of her. I'll come and see you as soon as I get my work done."

Frank went on board his vessel, where he was received by the officer of the deck, who showed him the way into the cabin. After the captain had indorsed his orders, he strolled leisurely about the ship, examining into every thing, for as yet he knew nothing of gun-boat life.

The Ticonderoga was a queer-looking craft. She was not exactly a Monitor; but she had a turret forward, and mounted two eleven-inch guns and four twelve-pounder howitzers. She had a heavy iron ram on her bow, and the turret was protected by three inches of iron, and the deck with two inches. It did not seem possible that a cannon-ball could make any impression on her thick armor.

The officers' quarters were all below decks; and, although it was then the middle of winter, Frank found it rather uncomfortable in his bunk.

During the two weeks that elapsed before the ship was ready to sail, the time was employed in getting every thing in order - in drilling at the great guns, and with muskets and broad-swords.

Most of the crew were old seamen, who understood their duty; and by the time their sailing orders came, every thing moved like clock-work.

In the mean time Frank had been assigned his station, which - being the youngest officer on board the ship - was to command the magazine. He learned very rapidly, and, as he was always attentive to his duties, he grew in favor with both officers and men.

At length, one afternoon, the anchor was weighed, and the Ticonderoga steamed down the river. Her orders were to report to the Admiral, who had sailed from Cairo about a week previous. They found him at Arkansas Post, where they arrived too late to take part in the fight. In a few days a station was assigned to her in the Mississippi River; and the Ticonderoga immediately set sail, in obedience to orders.

# CHAPTER VIII

## THE STRUGGLE BETWEEN THE LINES

One day, about two weeks after they came out of Arkansas River, the Ticonderoga stopped at Smith's Landing to take on wood, as her supply of coal had run short. The vessel was made fast to the bank, and, while the seamen were bringing in the wood, the paymaster's steward called Frank's attention to some cattle which were feeding on the bank, and remarked: "I wish we could go out and shoot one of them." "So do I," said Frank; "I've eaten salt pork until I am tired of it. Let's go and ask the captain."

"I'm agreed," said the steward.

The captain was walking on deck at the time and his permission was readily obtained, for he himself had grown tired of ship's pork; Frank, accompanied by the steward, and a seaman who was an expert butcher, started out. They were armed with muskets, and, as they were all good shots, and did not wish to kill more than enough to feed the ship's company once, they took with them no ammunition besides what was in the guns. At the place where the Ticonderoga was lying, the levee - an embankment about six feet high, built to prevent the water from overflowing - ran back into the woods about half a mile, then, making a bend like a horse-shoe, came back to the river again, inclosing perhaps a dozen acres of low, swampy land; and it was in this swamp that the cattle were. They proved to be very wild; but, after a considerable run, Frank

Harry Castlemon

succeeded in bringing down one, and the steward and seaman finally killed another. The question now was, how to get the meat on board the vessel. While they were debating on the matter, they were startled by the clatter of horses' hoofs on the levee; and, instead of drawing back into the bushes, out of sight, they very imprudently waited to see who the horsemen were. Presently, a party of guerrillas, to their utter amazement - for they had not dreamed that the rebels were so near them - galloped up.

The rebels discovered them at the same moment, and one of them exclaimed:

"I'll be dog-gone if thar ain't a Yank;" and, not knowing how many there might be of the "Yanks," they very prudently drew up their horses. One of them, however, who appeared to be the leader of the band, comprehended their situation at a glance, and exclaimed:

"Throw down your arms, and you shall be treated like men!"

This brought them to their senses, and they turned and ran for their lives. They had scarcely made a dozen steps before the bullets and buckshot began to rattle about their ears; but the trees and bushes were so thick that they escaped unhurt. Frank reached the vessel far in advance of the others; as he came over the side, panting and excited, the captain, who was still on deck, inquired:

"What's the matter, Mr. Nelson?"

"We ran foul of some guerrillas out there in the woods, sir," replied Frank.

"How many of them did you see?"

"They didn't give us much of a chance to judge of their numbers, sir; but I should say that there were at least a dozen of them, and they were coming this way. I shouldn't wonder if they intended to pick off some of the men who are carrying in wood."

"Mr. Hurd," said the captain, turning to the executive officer, "take thirty men, who are good shots, and go out there and keep those fellows off. Mr. Nelson will go with you."

Frank accordingly ran below, and armed himself with a revolver and musket, and buckled on a cartridge-box. When the men were ready, he led the way, along the levee, so that, if the guerrillas were advancing, they would be certain to meet them. But they saw no signs of them until they came within sight of a barn which stood in the woods, about a mile from the river. The rebels were gathered before it, as if in consultation, and greeted the approach of the sailors with a scattering volley of musketry, which whistled harmlessly over their heads, or plowed up the ground before them.

"Give 'em a shot, boys," said the executive officer, "and then scatter, and let each man take to a tree and fight Indian fashion."

The sailors wheeled into line with all the promptness and regularity of veteran troops; and before the smoke of their muskets cleared away, they had disappeared, like a flock of young partridges. The rebels had also treed, and the skirmish was continued for half an hour, without any damage being done to either party.

This style of fighting did not suit Frank, and he began to urge the executive officer to advance, and drive them from their position. But the officer did not think it safe to attempt it; for, although he had seen but a small number of the rebels, he did not know how many there might be hidden away in the bushes.

"Well, then," said Frank, after thinking a moment, "I have another proposition to make. If you will give me ten men, and engage the rebels warmly in front, I'll go and get that fresh beef."

"Where did you leave it?" inquired the officer.

"In the woods, about three hundred yards to the left of where the rebels now are."

"Very well; pick out your men, and go ahead."

Frank accordingly selected the boatswain's mate, an old, gray-headed man, who had been in the navy from boyhood, as his first lieutenant, and ordered him to call for volunteers.

If there is any thing a sailor admires, it is bravery in an officer. Every one on board the Ticonderoga, from the captain down, was acquainted with Frank's gallant behavior at Cypress Bend, although he himself had never said a word about it; and this, together with his uniform kindness toward the men under his command, and the respect he always showed his brother officers, had made him very popular with the ship's company; and when the mate - who was never better pleased than when he could do Frank a service-passed the word along the line that Mr. Nelson had called for volunteers, the men flocked around him in all directions. The mate quickly selected the required number, and Frank led them toward the place where they had left the beef.

The woods were very thick, and, of course, the rebels, who were hidden in the bushes, on the other side of the levee, knew nothing of what was going on. Frank sent two of his men to the levee, to watch the motions of the rebels, with orders not to fire unless they attempted to advance; and then pulled off his coat, and set to work, with the others, cutting up the beef. This was soon accomplished; and, after getting it all ready to carry to the vessel, Frank, after consulting with the mate, concluded that the rebels ought to be punished for what they had done, and he determined to try the effect of a cross-fire upon them.

He cautiously advanced his men to the levee, when he found that the rebels had been growing bolder; and one of them, who was mounted on a powerful iron-gray horse, would frequently ride out from his concealment, and advance toward the place where the men under the executive officer were stationed, coolly deliver his fire, and then retreat out of range of their guns, to reload.

"Now, boys," said Frank, "if that fellow tries that again, I'll put a stopper on his shooting for awhile."

The rebel, who, of course, was entirely ignorant of the proximity of Frank's party, soon reappeared, and rode rapidly down the levee, until he came directly opposite the place where Frank and his men were concealed, and then drew up his horse, and settled himself in his saddle, for a good shot. But at that instant the report of Frank's musket echoed through the woods, and the horse on which the rebel was mounted fell to the ground, with a bullet in his brain. Before the astonished guerrilla could extricate himself from the saddle, Frank, with more recklessness than prudence, had bounded out of his concealment, and seized him by the collar with one hand, at the same time attempting to draw his revolver with the other.

"You're my prisoner!" he exclaimed.

But the rebel had no sooner regained his feet, than he seized Frank around the body, and, lifting him from his feet, threw him heavily to the ground. Frank's revolver had become entangled in his belt in such a manner that he could not draw it, and he now saw how foolhardy he had been, for his antagonist was a man of almost twice his size, and possessed of enormous strength. But Frank still retained his presence of mind, and, in falling, he managed to catch the rebel by the hair, and pulled him to the ground with him. He clung to him with a death-grip, and the guerrilla, after trying in vain to break his hold, attempted to draw a knife from his belt. Frank seized it at the same moment, when each used all his skill and strength to obtain possession of it.

Both parties gazed in utter amazement, as this singular struggle went on and neither dared to fire a shot, for fear of hitting their own man. At length the mate, who, with his men, had watched the progress of the conflict, with their feelings worked up to the highest pitch of excitement, discovered that the rebel, by his superior strength, was gaining the advantage; and he knew that the only way to save his officer was to drive the rebels from their position.

"Steady there, lads!" he exclaimed; "fix bayonets."

The order was promptly obeyed.

"Ready, now! Aim! Fire! Charge bayonets! Forward, double-quick!"

The sailors broke from their concealment with a loud yell, and rushed toward the rebel line. They were soon overtaken by the men under command of the executive officer, who, not wishing to be outdone by their comrades, had come to their assistance.

The rebels were taken completely by surprise, and, after delivering a straggling fire, rapidly retreated.

The charge made by the sailors infused new courage into Frank, who increased his exertions, and struggled furiously for the possession of the knife.

"Hold on," exclaimed the rebel; "I'll surrender, if you will promise me kind treatment."

"I guess you'll surrender any way," said Frank; "and you may be sure that you will be well treated."

"Let go my hair, then," said the rebel; "and let me get up."

Frank accordingly released his hold, and the rebel rose to his feet, and was immediately seized by the mate, who, with his men, was just returning from the pursuit of the rebels.

After the prisoner had delivered up his weapons, they marched back to the place where they had left the beef, and then started for the vessel.

Every one was soon made acquainted with the particulars of the fight, and Frank was again the hero of the mess-room.

# CHAPTER IX

## A UNION FAMILY

After two days' sail, the Ticonderoga arrived at Phillips's Landing, where she had been ordered to take her station; for the Admiral had received information that the rebel General Marmaduke was preparing to cross the river, with his forces, at that place.

They came to anchor in front of a large plantation, owned by the man after whom the place was named. In a short time, a boat, rowed by two stout negroes, and which contained two ladies and a gentleman, came alongside.

The captain received them, as they came upon the quarter-deck, and the gentleman, after introducing himself as Mr. Phillips, and apologizing for the liberty they had taken in coming on board, asked if the captain could furnish them with some Northern papers. They lived in an out-of-the-way place, he said, where boats seldom landed, for fear of the guerrillas, and they were entirely ignorant of what was going on.

The captain seemed much pleased with his visitors. After complying with their request, he conducted them down into the cabin, where they passed an hour in conversation. When they were about to take their departure, they invited the captain and his officers to call on them, and assured them that there were no rebels in the vicinity.

The captain was an old sailor, and had been in the service so long that he was inclined to be suspicious of any thing that looked like friendship on the part of a person living in an enemy's country. But, after calling on Mr. Phillips's family a few times, without discovering any thing to confirm his suspicions, he allowed both officers and men to go ashore at all times; and soon quite an intimacy sprung up between them and the people of the plantation, and dinner parties and horse-back rides were the order of the day.

Frank had been elected caterer of his mess, and as he was obliged to furnish provisions, he had a good excuse for being ashore most of his time. He became a regular visitor at the plantation, and was soon well acquainted with each member of the family. They all professed to be unconditional Union people, with the exception of the youngest daughter, who boldly stated that her sympathies were, and always had been, with the South; and she and Frank had many a long argument about the war.

Things went on thus for a considerable time, when, early one morning, as Frank was on his way to the plantation, to buy his marketing, a negro met him, as he was ascending the hill that led to the quarters, and said:

"I'd like to speak just one word with you, young master."

"Well, what is it, uncle?" said Frank; "talk away."

"Let us move on, this way first, for I don't want them to see us from the house."

Frank followed the negro behind one of the cabins, and the latter continued:

"I'm afraid you and all the officers on your boat will be captured one of these days."

"What do you mean?" inquired Frank, in surprise, half

inclined to think that the negro was crazy.

"I suppose you don't know that my master and mistress, and all the white folks on the plantation, are rebels, do you?"

"No; and I don't believe they are."

"Yes, they are. My master is a Major in the rebel army; and that Miss Annie you come to see every day has got a sweetheart in the army, and she tells him every thing you say. Besides, they send a mail across the river, here, twice every month. I took one across myself, night before last."

"I believe you're lying to me, you old rascal," exclaimed Frank.

"No, young master," answered the negro; "every word I have told you is gospel truth. You see, my daughter waits on Miss Annie, and I find out every thing."

"You say Miss Phillips has a sweetheart in the army?"

"Yes; and he was here to see her not long ago. He is a lieutenant, and has gone up to Conway's Point, with two cannons, to fire into steamers. His name is Miller; and you would know him from a long scar on his left cheek. Wasn't Miss Annie on board your boat two days ago?"

"Yes, I believe so."

"Well, she stole a book."

"A book!" repeated Frank. "What kind of a book?"

"I don't know the name of it. It was a small book, and had lead fastened to the covers."

"By gracious!" exclaimed Frank, "that was the captain's signal-book."

"Yes; she told my daughter that she took it out of the captain's room."

Frank did not stop to buy any marketing, but hastily catching up his basket, he hurried back to the vessel.

"Orderly," he exclaimed, as he approached the marine who always stood at the cabin door, "ask the captain if I may see him."

"He hasn't got up yet, sir."

"That makes no difference. Tell him that I have something particular to say to him."

The orderly went into the cabin, and, in a few moments, returned, and said:

"The captain says walk in, sir."

"Captain," said Frank, after he had closed the door carefully behind him, "have you lost your signal-book?"

"No, I guess not;" answered the captain, in a tone of surprise. "What makes you ask?"

"I heard, a few moments ago, that it had been stolen from you."

"I have not had occasion to use it for two or three weeks," answered the captain, getting out of bed; "but I know exactly where I put it;" and he opened a drawer in the sideboard, and commenced to overhaul the contents.

"Set me down for a landlubber," he exclaimed, at length, "if it hasn't been stolen. It isn't here, at any rate."

Frank then related the conversation which had taken place between himself and the negro, and the captain continued:

"Well, I always thought those folks had some object in view, or they would not have been so friendly. I can't reproach myself for neglecting my duty, for I watched them pretty closely."

"I wonder how that girl knew that the signal-book was in that drawer," said Frank.

"I suppose she must have seen me put it in there," said the captain. "Now, the question is, now to go to work to recover it. It will do no good to search the house."

"If you will leave the matter in my hands, sir," said Frank, "I will agree to recover the signal-book, and capture that mail-bag which they intend to send across the river in a few days."

"Well," said the captain, "it was you who first knew that the signal-book was gone, and I believe you ought to have the honor of sifting the matter to the bottom. Find out all you can, and call on me for any assistance you may need."

Frank immediately returned to the plantation, and started toward the quarters, in quest of the negro who had given him the information, whom he found chopping wood in front of one of the cabins.

"See here, uncle," he exclaimed, "I want you to keep me posted on all that goes on here on the plantation; and tell your daughter to find out when that rebel lieutenant is coming here again, and when they intend to send that mail across the river."

"I will do my best, young master," answered the negro. "But you won't tell any one what I have said to you? I shall be killed, sure, if you do"

"No, uncle, I shan't betray you; so don't be afraid," said Frank; and, after purchasing some articles which they needed in the mess, he returned on board the boat.

A week passed on, but nothing further was developed. The

officers of the vessel still continued to visit the plantation, and Mr. Phillips and his family always seemed glad to see them, and evidently did all in their power to make their visits agreeable.

As soon as Frank had time to think the matter over, he wondered why he had not known that something suspicious was going on. He remembered now that Mr. Phillips had often questioned him closely concerning the manner in which the gun-boats were stationed along the river, and the distance they were apart. And he thought of other questions which had been asked him by the family, which, although they did not seem strange at the time, now seemed suspicious. At first he had been inclined to doubt the negro's story; but his doubts were soon removed by the appearance of a transport, which was completely riddled with shot; and her captain reported that they had been fired into by a battery of two guns, at Conway's Point. Frank knew that it was the work of the rebel lieutenant, and he hoped that it would soon be his fortune to meet him face to face.

One evening, just after supper, the negro appeared on the bank, with some chickens in his hand, which was a signal to Frank that he had something to communicate. He immediately set off alone, in a skiff. When he reached the shore, the negro informed him that the rebel lieutenant was expected at the plantation that evening, and that he would bring with him the mail, which was to be carried across the river at midnight.

After paying the negro for his chickens, in order to deceive any one who might be watching them, Frank returned to the vessel, and informed the captain that, if he would give him twenty men, he would fulfill his promise. He did not acquaint him with what he had learned, however, for fear that the captain would send an officer with him, and thus rob him of the laurels now almost within his grasp.

As soon as it was dark, Frank picked out the men he wished to accompany him, and started off. His first care was to quietly surround the house, after he had placed his men to his satisfaction, he removed his sword, thrust a brace of revolvers into his pocket, and walked up and knocked at the door. It was opened by the youngest of the girls, who started back and turned pale when she saw the young officer; but instantly recovering her presence of mind, she exclaimed:

"Good evening, Mr. Nelson; walk in. Allow me to introduce to you my cousin, Mr. Williams," she continued, as they entered the parlor.

As she spoke, a tall, handsome young man rose from his seat, and made a low bow. It was none other than Lieutenant Miller; for there was the scar on his cheek, which had been described to him by the negro.

After returning the rebel's salutation, Frank seated himself on the sofa, and said:

"I shall trouble you only a moment. I merely came here on a little matter of business. I understand that there is a rebel mail to be carried across the river, from this house, to-night."

The suddenness with which this announcement was made was astounding. Mrs. Phillips appeared ready to faint; Annie turned very pale; and the lieutenant raised his hand to his breast, as if about to draw a weapon.

"What do you mean, sir?" inquired Mr. Phillips, with well-feigned surprise.

"I mean," answered Frank, "that, since we anchored opposite this house, we have been associating with the worst kind of rebels. Put down your hand, Lieutenant Miller! If I see you make that move again, I shall be obliged to shoot you. You have professed to be Union people," continued Frank, settling himself back in his seat, and coolly crossing his legs, "and have been treated as such; you have, however, attempted to betray us, by communicating such of our plans and movements as you could learn to the rebels. But you have been discovered at last. You, gentlemen, will please consider yourselves my prisoners. Miss Phillips, have the kindness to produce that mail-bag, and the signal-book you took from the captain. If you refuse, I shall be obliged to take you on board the ship, as a prisoner."

The girl saw that there was no alternative, and she pulled from under the sofa, where Frank sat, the mail-bag, which appeared to be well filled with letters, and dispatched a servant to her room after the signal-book, which was to have been sent across the river with the mail.

After Frank had relieved the lieutenant of his weapons, he called two of his men into the house, and, after delivering the prisoners into their charge, returned to the vessel.

That evening the captain examined the mail, and found several letters which showed, beyond a doubt, that their prisoners were connected with the rebel army; and they were, accordingly, sent to the Admiral, on the first steamer that went up the river.

About two weeks afterward, the captain of the Ticonderoga received orders to proceed with his vessel to Helena, and take command of an expedition which was preparing to start down the Yazoo Pass. They found the fleet, consisting of the Manhattan, six "tin-clads," and several transports, loaded with troops, assembled in Moon Lake, which was about six miles from the Mississippi River; and, on the 23d day of February, they entered the pass, the Ticonderoga leading the way.

The west shore of Moon Lake was bounded by a swamp, through which ran the pass, which was just wide enough to admit one good-sized vessel. It was filled with trees, which stood so close together that it seemed impossible to work a passage through them; and the men on deck were constantly in danger of being killed by falling limbs. They advanced slowly, sometimes making not more than four miles in a day; and it was almost two weeks before they reached Coldwater River.

# CHAPTER X

## A SPUNKY REBEL

In the afternoon of the day of their arrival, the Ticonderoga tied up in front of a large plantation-house. As soon as the vessel was made fast to the bank, the captain turned to the executive officer, and exclaimed:

"Mr. Smith, please call away one company of small-armed men. Mr. Nelson," he continued, turning to Frank, "I wish you to take command of the company, and go ashore and search that house for fire-arms, and bring on board all you find."

"Very good, sir," answered Frank; and he hurried down to his room to buckle on his sword and revolver.

In a few minutes the company was formed on deck, and Frank marched them out on the bank and then up to the house. His first care was to surround the building, so that, in case there were any men in it, their escape would be entirely cut off. He then, in company with the boatswain's mate and two men, walked up and knocked at the door. After some delay, the summons was answered by a negro woman, who scowled upon him, and waited for him to make known his wants.

"Is your master or mistress in?" inquired Frank.

"Yes, missus is h'ar," answered the woman, gruffly.

"Well, I should like to see her."

"Den you stay h'ar, an' I'll ax her if she wants to see you."

"No, aunty, that won't do. I must see her, whether she wants to see me or not;" and Frank unceremoniously entered the house, followed by his men.

"Now, where is your mistress, aunty?" he inquired.

"She's up stairs," answered the woman.

"Well, then," said Frank, turning to the boatswain's mate, "you come with me, and let the others remain here until we return."

Frank then ascended the stairs, and very easily found his way to the room where the lady was; and, as he entered, he politely removed his cap.

"Well, sir," said the lady, in no very pleasant tone, "what do you wish?"

"I have been ordered to come here and search your house for fire-arms," replied Frank.

"I suppose I shall be obliged to submit to it, for I have not the power to prevent you; if I had, I should certainly use it. But, I hope you will be gentleman enough not to steal every thing we have in the house."

Frank's face reddened to the very roots of his hair at this insult, and he replied, in a voice choked with indignation:

"No, madam, we shall disturb nothing. I hope you do not take us for thieves;" and he turned and tried a door, (several of which opened off the room in which the lady was sitting), but it was fastened on the other side.

"That's a bed-room," exclaimed the lady, angrily. "I hope you are not going in there!"

"Certainly I am, madam. I am going into every nook and corner of your house. My orders were to search your building, and I intend to obey them. Is there any one in here?"

"Yes, sir; my daughters are in there."

"Then, why don't they open this door?" and Frank, who was getting out of patience, pounded loudly upon the door with the butt of his revolver.

"Is that you, mother?" inquired a voice from the room.

"No," answered Frank, "it isn't mother; but open this door."

"Yes, in a minute."

"Open this door immediately," repeated Frank, who began to suspect that he had been purposely delayed.

But the persons in the room made no reply; when the boatswain's mate, at a sign from Frank, raised his foot, and, with one kick of his heavy boot, sent the door from its hinges. Loud screams issued from the room, which, as Frank entered, he found to be occupied by two young ladies, who, judging from the overturned work-basket, and the half-finished articles of apparel which were scattered about over the floor, had been engaged in sewing.

"Don't be alarmed, ladies," said Frank, "you shall not be harmed. Jack," he continued, turning to the boatswain's mate, "just examine that bed."

"Oh, don't," exclaimed one of the young ladies, "don't, for mercy's sake. Do go away from here."

"Ellen," exclaimed her mother, who had followed Frank into

the room, "don't make a child of yourself. I am surprised at you."

"We shall leave every thing just as we find it," said Frank, who was a good deal surprised at the conduct of the girl. "All we want is the fire-arms, if you have any in the house."

"Yes, we have got some here," said Ellen, "and I will get them for you;" and she drew out from the bed-clothes two beauti-fully-finished rifles, a quantity of ammunition, a cavalry sword, and a double-barreled shot-gun. "There," she exclaimed, as she handed them to Frank; "there are no more in this room. Now, do go away."

"Ellen," said her mother, who was evidently very anxious about the girl's conduct, "will you keep quiet?"

"Don't say any thing to him, Ellen," said her sister, whose name was Mary; "don't ask any favors of a Yankee. Let him stay here till doomsday if" -

She was interrupted by a loud scream from Ellen; and the mate, who had been "reconnoitering" under the bed, exclaimed:

"Here you are! Come out o' that, you son of a sea-cook;" and he seized something which struggled and fought furiously, but all to no purpose, for the mate soon pulled into sight tall man, dressed in the uniform of a rebel officer.

Ellen screamed and cried louder than ever, and even her mother could not refrain from shedding tears; but Mary, although pale as death, retained her haughty look, and was evidently too proud to manifest any feeling in the presence of a Federal officer.

"I knowed there was something of this kind goin' on, sir," said Jack, turning to his officer, and giving his pants a hitch; "I knowed, by the way the young lady handed over them we'pons, that there was something about that bed she didn't want us to see."

"Yes, Ellen," said the rebel, "I have to thank you for my capture. If it hadn't been for your crying and whimpering, I might have" -

"Escaped," exclaimed Jack. "No, sir; not so easy. Don't go to jawin' her, now, 'cause yer ketched. Come, now," he continued, "let's have yer we'pons."

The rebel coolly handed out two silver-mounted revolvers, which the mate thrust into his belt.

"Now, I hope you're satisfied," said Mary, impatiently; "and are ready to go and leave us in peace."

"Not quite," answered Frank. "I have not yet obeyed my orders. As I said before, I must see the inside of every room in your house. Jack, send two men on board the ship with that prisoner."

"Ay, ay, sir," answered the mate, touching his cap. "Come, you corn-fed, march."

The mother and sisters of the rebel crowded around him, to say good-by; and, in spite of the unladylike, and even insulting manner with which they had treated him, Frank could not help pitying them.

When the mate had seen the prisoner safe on the boat, he went back, and Frank continued his search. But no more weapons or prisoners being found, he and his men returned on board, well satisfied with their success.

After supper, as Frank was walking up and down the deck, arm in arm with one of his brother officers, the orderly approached, and, touching his cap, informed him that the captain wished to see him.

"Mr. Nelson," said the captain, as Frank entered the cabin, "come here."

Frank followed the captain to one of the after windows, and the latter inquired:

"Do you see *that*?"

Frank looked in the direction indicated by the captain, and was surprised to see a rebel flag floating from one of the windows of the house.

"Yes, sir; I see it," said Frank.

"Well, sir, go over there, and tell those women to have that flag taken in and sent on board this ship. Don't touch it yourself: they put it out there, and they must take it in. That's a pretty piece of impudence, indeed - a rebel flag floating in the breeze in the face of a Federal vessel of war!" and the eccentric captain paced up and down his cabin, in a state of considerable excitement.

Frank started off, and in a few moments again stood before the mistress of the house.

"You're here again, sir, are you?" she asked, petulantly.

"Yes, ma'am," replied Frank, not the least annoyed by the tone in which he was addressed, or the sharp glances which the ladies threw at him, "I'm here; and I came to tell you that the captain wishes you to have that rebel flag removed from your window, and sent on board the ship."

"Is there any thing else your captain wants?" inquired Mary, with a sneer.

"No, ma'am, not at present; but he wishes that flag taken down immediately."

The ladies made no reply. After a moment's pause, Frank inquired:

"Do you intend to comply with his orders?"

"I did not put the flag up there," said the mother.

"It makes no difference who put it up there, madam," said Frank, warmly, "it must come down; and I would advise you not to hesitate long, for the captain is not one who can be trifled with."

As Frank ceased speaking, Mary touched a signal-bell, which stood on the table near her. A servant appeared almost instantly, and the young lady said:

"Show this man out."

Frank, who saw that it would do no good to remain, put on his cap and followed the servant down stairs.

"Well, what did they say?" inquired the captain, when Frank again entered the cabin.

"They didn't say any thing, sir," replied Frank. "They neither said they would, nor they would not, take it down."

Frank was careful not to say a word about the manner in which they had treated him, for he knew it would only irritate the captain, and make matters worse.

"They didn't say whether they would take it down or not, eh!" exclaimed the captain. "Please help yourself to a chair, Mr. Nelson, and, in a few moments, I will give you your orders."

Frank accordingly took a seat, and the captain stationed himself at the window, with his watch in his hand. Frank knew by this that the captain had granted the rebels a few moments' grace; and he also knew that, unless the flag came down soon, and was sent on board the vessel, something unpleasant would happen. At length the allotted time expired, and the captain said:

"Mr. Nelson, take a dozen men, and go ashore. Give those women just ten minutes to remove their furniture, and then fire the house. No building shall float a secesh flag, and stand, while I have the power to burn it."

This time the ladies made no remark when Frank entered the room where they were sitting, for they knew by his looks that they were about to receive the punishment their folly merited.

"Madam," said Frank, speaking in a tone which showed how much he dreaded to break the intelligence, "I am ordered to burn your house."

"Yes," answered the mother, bitterly; "I expected that to be your next errand. I suppose your brutal captain will feel perfectly satisfied when he sees us deprived of a home."

"I thought the Yankees were too gallant to make war on women and children," chimed in Mary. "That has always been their boast," continued she, very spitefully.

"So they are," replied Frank. "But the captain is one who will not tolerate an exhibition of treason in any one, be it man, woman, or child. You have no one to blame but yourselves. But we have no time to waste in argument. I will give you ten minutes in which to remove your furniture and will assist you, if you wish it."

"We can take care of ourselves," said the mother. "No one asked you for assistance."

Frank made no reply; and the ladies, assisted by their servants, immediately commenced the removal of the most valuable articles; and when the time had expired, a straw-bed was pulled into the middle of the floor, a match was applied to it, and the house was soon enveloped in flames.

Frank could not help pitying the women, who were thus obliged to stand by and witness the destruction of their home. But he knew that they had brought it on themselves, and that they deserved it; and, besides, he had only done his duty, for he was acting under orders.

The women, however, did not seem to be in the least concerned; for when the roof fell in with a crash, Mary commenced the rebel air, "Bonnie Blue Flag," and sang it through to the end. Frank admired her "spunk," even though her sympathies were enlisted in a bad cause.

He remained until the house was entirely consumed, and then returned on board his vessel.

# CHAPTER XI

## FRANK A PRISONER

In the afternoon of the following day, while it was Frank's watch on deck, as the Ticonderoga came suddenly around an abrupt bend in the river, a puff of smoke rose from behind an embankment, about half a mile in advance, while a shell whistled over the vessel, and dropped into the water without exploding.

Frank immediately requested the pilot to blow four whistles, which was a signal to the other boats that they were attacked; and, after sending the messenger-boy below to report to the captain, he raised his glass to his eye, and found that they were directly in front of a good-sized fort, built of cotton bales and embankments, and mounting at least five heavy guns. A flag-staff rose from the center of the fort, and supported the "stars and bars," which flaunted defiantly in the breeze. This was Fort Pemberton, the only formidable fortification the rebels had between the Mississippi and Yazoo Rivers.

The captain came on deck immediately, and ordered the vessel to be stopped; and, when the other boats came up, they were ordered to take their stations along the bank, on each side of the river, out of range of the guns of the fort. When the entire fleet had assembled, the Ticonderoga, in company with the Manhattan, steamed down, and opened fire on the fort, with a view to ascertain its strength. The fort replied vigorously, and, after an hour's firing, the vessels withdrew.

The next morning, at an early hour, the troops were landed, but, for some reason, it was afternoon before they were ready to march. At three o'clock they were drawn up in line in the woods, about two miles from the fort, where the men stacked arms, and stretched themselves out in the shade of the trees.

In the mean time the iron-clads had been preparing for the fight. The magazines were opened and lighted; the casemates covered with a coat of grease, to glance the shot which might strike them; the men were at their stations, and when all was ready, they steamed down toward the fort, the Ticonderoga leading the way.

Frank, by attention to his duties, had rapidly learned the gun-drill, and had been promoted to the command of one of the guns in the turret. He thought he had become quite accustomed to the noise of bullets, but he could not endure the silence that then reigned in the ship. The men, stripped to the waist, stood at their guns as motionless as so many statues; and, although Frank tried hard to exhibit the same indifference that they did, his mind was exceedingly busy, and it seemed to him that he thought of every thing he had done during his life. Oh, how he longed to hear the order passed to commence firing! Any thing was preferable to that awful stillness.

At length, the captain came into the turret, where he always took his station in action, and glanced hastily at the counte-nance of each of the officers and men. He seemed satisfied with his examination, for he immediately took his stand where he could see all that was going on, and gave orders to the pilot to head the vessel directly toward the fort; and then every thing relapsed into that horrible silence again. But this did not continue long; for, the moment they came within range, the fort opened on them, and a solid shot struck the casemate directly over Frank's gun, with a force that seemed to shake the entire vessel. Frank glanced at the captain, and saw him standing with his elbow on the starboard gun, and his head resting on his hand, watching the fort as coolly as though they had been engaged only in target practice.

The shells from the fort continued to fall around them, but the captain neither changed his position nor gave the order to fire. The port-holes in the turret were all closed, with the exception of the one at which the captain stood, and, of course, no one could see what was going on. Frank began to grow impatient. He did not like the idea of being shot at in that manner without returning the fire. At length the captain inquired:

"What have you in your gun, Mr. Nelson?"

"A five-second shell, sir," answered Frank, promptly.

"Very well. Run out your gun and give them a shot."

The men sprang to their stations in an instant; the ports flew open with a crash, and the heavy gun was ran out as easily as though it had been a twelve-pounder. The first captain seized the lock string; there was a deafening report, and an eleven-inch shell went booming into the fort. The force of the discharge ran the gun back into the turret again, and the ports closed as if by magic. They did not close entirely, however, for there was a space of about four inches left between them, to allow for the action of the rammer in loading. The gun was sponged, the cartridge driven home, and the gunner's mate stood at the muzzle of the gun, removing the cap from a shell, when a percussion shell from the fort struck in the space between the shutters and exploded. The discharge set fire to the shell which the gunner's mate was holding in his hand, and the unfortunate man was blown almost to atoms.

In naval actions there is nothing which will carry such terror and dismay among a ship's company as the bursting of one of their own shells; and the scene which followed the explosion in the turret of the Ticonderoga beggars all description. Old seamen, who had been in many a hard-fought battle, and had stood at their guns under the most deadly fire the enemy could pour upon them, without flinching, now deserted their stations, and ran about through the blinding and suffocating smoke that filled the turret, with blanched cheeks, trampling each other under their feet, and utterly disregarding the commands of their officers, who ran among them with drawn swords, and endeavored to force them back to their guns. It was some time before quiet was restored, and then Frank found, to his horror, that, out of twenty-five men which had composed his gun's crew, only ten were left. Four had been instantly killed, and eleven badly wounded. The deck was slippery with blood, and the turret was completely covered with it. The shrieks and groans of the wounded and dying were awful. Frank had never before witnessed such a scene, and, for a moment, he was so sick he could scarcely stand. But he had no time to waste in giving away to his feelings. After seeing the dead and wounded carried below, he returned to his station, and, with what was left of his gun's crew, fought bravely during the remainder of the action.

The fight continued until after dark, when the captain, knowing that it would be impossible to capture the fort without the assistance of the troops, ordered a retreat.

That same night a consultation of the naval and military commanders was held, and it was decided to renew the attack on the following morning. A battery of two thirty-pounder Parrotts was taken off one of the "tin-clads" and mounted on the bank, about half a mile back in the woods, and a mile from the fort. Captain Wilson, who commanded one of the mosquito boats, was ordered to take command of it, and Frank, at his own request, was permitted to accompany him as his aid. He started early the next morning with fifty men, who had been detailed from the gun-boats, and at sunrise was at his station.

The battery was masked, and the rebels knew nothing of its existence. The captain's orders were, not to fire until they heard the action opened by the iron-clads. Twenty-eight men were required to man the guns, and the others, armed with Spencer rifles, were to act as sharp-shooters. Frank, to his surprise, soon learned that this was all the support they were to have, the troops having been ordered to take the same station they had occupied the day before, and to hold themselves in readiness to charge upon the fort, as soon as the iron-clads had silenced the guns.

About ten o'clock the fort commenced firing, and Frank knew that the gun-boats were again under way. At length a loud report, which he could have recognized among a thousand, blended with the others, and, in obedience to the order of the captain, the men tore away the bushes which had masked the battery, and the fight became general.

Frank directed his fire upon a pile of cotton-bales, which protected one of the largest guns of the fort; but, as fast as he knocked them down, the rebels would recklessly spring out of the fort and put them up again. At length Captain Wilson ordered she sharp-shooters to advance five hundred yards nearer the fort. The rebels soon discovered this, and the cotton-bales were allowed to remain where they had fallen.

In half an hour that part of the fort was completely demolished; and the rebels, being without protection against the sharp-shooters, were obliged to abandon the gun.

While Frank was congratulating himself on the fine shooting he had done, and wondering why the troops were not ordered to charge, he was startled by the rapid report of muskets behind him. Three of his men fell dead where they had stood; and Frank turned just in time to see a party of rebels issuing from the woods. They came on with loud yells; and one of them, who appeared to be the leader, called out:

"Surrender, now, you infernal Yankees. Shoot down the first one who resists or attempts to escape," he added, turning to his men. "Stand to your guns, my lads!" shouted Captain Wilson. "Don't give ground an inch."

The sailors, always accustomed to obedience, gathered around their officers, and poured a murderous fire upon the advancing enemy, from their revolvers. The rebels, who were greatly superior in numbers, returned the fire, and the captain fell, mortally wounded. But the sailors stubbornly stood their ground, until the rebels closed up about them, and Frank saw that escape was impossible. But he fought like a young tiger, and determined that he would die before he would surrender; for even death was preferable to a long confinement in a Southern prison.

"Drop that pistol!" exclaimed a rebel, pointing his rifle directly at Frank's head, "or I'll blow your brains out."

"Blow away!" exclaimed Frank, seizing the rebel's rifle, with a quick movement, and firing his revolver full in his face; "I'll never surrender as long as I have strength left to stand on my feet. Give it to 'em, lads!"

The next moment Frank was prostrated by a severe blow on the head from the butt of a musket, and the sailors, finding that both their officers were gone, lost all heart, and threw down their weapons.

The rebels had scarcely time to collect their prisoners and retreat, when the troops, who had heard the noise of the conflict, and started to the rescue, arrived. But they were too late; for in less than half an hour Frank and his men were safe in the fort, and confined under guard.

# CHAPTER XII

## THE ESCAPE

Frank, as may be supposed, was not at all pleased with the prospect before him. He had often heard escaped prisoners relate sad stories of the treatment they had received while in the hands of the rebels; and, as he knew that they cherished an especial hatred toward gun-boatmen, he could not hope to fare very well.

The place where he was confined was in the lower part of the fort, directly in range of the shells from the iron-clads, and Frank expected to be struck by them every moment, for the pieces flew about him in all directions. Oh, how he prayed that the fort might be taken! He could see that one of their heaviest guns was dismounted, and a large detail of men was constantly occupied in carrying off the dead and wounded.

The firing continued until four o'clock in the afternoon, and then the gun-boats suddenly withdrew. The rebels cheered loudly as they disappeared around a bend in the river, and Frank gave up all hope: nothing now remained for him but a long captivity.

That evening, as soon as it was dark, he, with the other prisoners, was marched on board the General Quitman, a large steamer, lying just below the fort, and carried to Haines' Bluff, and from thence they went by rail to Vicksburg. Here Frank was separated from his men, and confined, for two days, with several army officers, in a small room in the jail. Early on the third morning he was again taken out, and sent across the river, into Louisiana, with about three hundred others. Their destination, he soon learned, was Tyler, a small town in Texas, where most of the Union prisoners captured in Mississippi were confined.

They were guarded by a battalion of cavalry, under command of the notorious Colonel Harrison, who called themselves the "Louisiana Wild-cats." Frank had never before seen this noted regiment, and he found that they were very appropriately named; for a more ferocious looking set of men he had never met. They all wore long hair and whiskers; and their faces looked as though they had never been acquainted with soap and water. They were armed with rifles, Bowie-knives, and revolvers, and seemed to take pleasure in boasting of the number of women and children and unarmed men they had slain.

They had not made more than a day's march, when Frank found that his troubles were just commencing. He was not accustomed to marching, and his feet soon became so swollen that he could scarcely stand on them. The heat was almost intolerable; the roads were very dusty, and the places where they were allowed to obtain water were many miles apart. Besides, as if to add to their sufferings, the rebels were continually stealing from the prisoners, and, finally, some of them were left with scarcely any clothing; and if the poor fellows ventured to remonstrate against such treatment, they were shot or bayoneted on the spot.

On the fourth day of the march, Frank noticed a soldier, just in advance of him, who was so weak that he could scarcely keep his feet. He had been wounded in the arm, at the late battle before Vicksburg, but not the least notice had been taken of it by the rebels, and he was suffering the most intense agony. Frank, although scarcely able to sustain himself, owing to the swollen condition of his feet, offered his assistance, which the poor fellow was glad enough to accept. But he continued to grow weaker every moment, and, finally, in spite of Frank's exertions, fell prostrate in the road.

"What's the matter here?" inquired the colonel, who happened to be riding by.

"This man isn't able to go any further," replied Frank.

"Then he doesn't need any of your help, you young Abolitionist; get back to your place! Here, Stiles," he continued, beckoning to one of his men and bending upon him a glance of peculiar meaning, "you stay here until this man dies."

The colonel rode up to the head of the column again, and Frank was obliged to move on with the others. But he could not relieve his mind of a feeling that something more dreadful than any thing he had yet seen was about to take place. He frequently turned and looked back, and saw the man lying where he had fallen, and the rebel, who had dismounted from his horse, standing over him, leaning on his rifle. At length a bend in the road hid them from sight. In a few moments, Frank heard the report of a gun, and presently the rebel rode up, with the coat, pants, and boots which had once belonged to the soldier, hanging on his arm. Such scenes as this were enacted every day; but, for some unaccountable reason, Frank was not molested, beyond having his boots stolen one night while he was asleep. He had made up his mind that he would escape at the first opportunity; but he was in no condition to travel, and, besides, the sight of several ferocious bloodhounds, which accompanied the rebels, was enough to deter him from making the attempt.

After a march of two weeks, during which he suffered more than he had thought it possible for him to endure, they arrived at Shreveport. Here they encamped for the night, with the understanding that they were to start for Tyler - which was one hundred and ten miles further on - early the next morning. Frank concluded that he had walked about far enough. "If I intend to escape," he soliloquized, "I might as well start from here as from Tyler. I'll play off sick, and see if I can't get them to leave me here; and then, as soon as I become strong enough to travel, I'll be missed some fine day."

Accordingly, the next morning, when the prisoners were ordered to "fall in," Frank did not stir; and, when the sergeant came to arouse him, he appeared to be in the greatest agony. So well did he play his part, that the doctor declared that it was impossible for him to go on; and he was accordingly left behind. As soon as the prisoners had gone, he was carried to the hospital, which was a large brick building, standing on the outskirts of the town. The lower floor was used as a barrack for the soldiers who guarded the building, and the upper rooms as a hospital and guard-house. Frank found about fifteen Federal soldiers, and as many rebels, who were confined for various offenses, principally desertion.

Frank soon became acquainted with his fellow-prisoners, and the stories they told of their treatment made the cold sweat start out all over him; but when he spoke of escape, he was surprised to find that there was not one among them who dared to make the attempt. But this did not alter his determination. He resolved that, rather than remain in prison, he would go alone. He grew stronger every day, and succeeded in securing a pair of shoes, and a compass, for which he gave the last shirt he had. His determination was to take to the woods, until he had escaped pursuit, and then strike for Red River. He knew that this route would bring him out a good distance below Vicksburg, but still it would be easier and safer than traveling across the country; and he hoped that the rebel stronghold would be taken by the time he reached the Mississippi River.

Finally, one dark night - after he had well matured his plans – he concluded to make the trial. So, waiting until every one in the room appeared to be asleep - for he had been told that there were some who must know nothing of his intention - he carefully raised one of the windows, and looked out. He had made all his observations beforehand, and knew that the window was about twenty feet above the ground. He had tried in vain to obtain a rope strong enough to assist him in his descent; and his only alternative was, to hang by his hands and "drop" to the ground, where, he hoped, aided by the darkness, to escape the fire of the guards.

He was crawling noiselessly out of the window, when he was startled by the creaking of the stairs, as if some one was descending them; and, at the same time, hasty footsteps sounded under the window. Frank saw that he had been discovered, and, hastily climbing back into the room, he closed the window and threw himself on the floor, and appeared to be fast asleep.

"Very well done!" exclaimed an officer, who suddenly appeared at the top of the stairs. "Very well done, indeed. Now, you young Yankee, I don't want to see you try that move again. If you do, I shall be obliged to shoot you. Do you understand?"

Frank replied in the affirmative; and the officer, after satisfying himself that the prisoners were all in the room, went below again, leaving a guard at the head of the stairs, who kept a close watch upon Frank until morning.

He was a good deal annoyed and perplexed at the unsuccessful termination of his adventure; but he could not make up his mind what it was that had led to his discovery. Still, he was not discouraged; but, in spite of the officer's warning, determined to renew his attempt at escape, as soon as an opportunity was offered.

The next day, while he was eating his scanty dinner, the lieutenant in charge of the prisoners came in, and, as was his custom, began to argue with them as to the probable termination of the war. Frank had always hoped that he would let him alone, for the lieutenant invariably became enraged if the prisoners endeavored to uphold their Government.

"Well, young man," he exclaimed, walking up to Frank, "how

Harry Castlemon

do you get along?"

"As well as can be expected, I suppose," answered Frank.

"How do you relish being a prisoner? Are you not sorry that you ever took up arms against us?"

"No, I am not," answered Frank, indignantly, "You'll have to fight me again, as soon as I get out of this scrape."

"What made you come down here to fight us?"

"Because I thought you needed a good drubbing."

"Well, we haven't had it yet;" said the lieutenant, stroking his moustache. "Why didn't you take Fort Pemberton? You got the worst of it there. We sunk the Ticonderoga."

"Oh, yes," answered Frank, with a sneer, "no doubt of it. But, on the whole, I think you had better tell that to the marines."

"You don't believe it, then! Well, how do you think this war is going to end?"

"Now, see here," said Frank, "I wish you would travel on, and let me alone. I am a prisoner, and in your power; and I don't want to be abused for speaking my mind; for, if I answer your questions at all, I shall say just what I think."

"That is what I like," said the lieutenant. "You need not be afraid to speak your mind freely. Now, tell me, how do you think this struggle will end?"

"There is only one way for it to end, and that is in your subjugation."

"But what is your object in fighting us?"

"To preserve the Union!"

"You're a liar!" shouted the lieutenant. "You're fighting to free the niggers."

"Well, have it your own way," answered Frank. "But, if I'm a liar, you're a gentleman, so take it and go on. You need not ask me any more questions, for I shan't answer them."

The lieutenant muttered something about hanging every Yankee he could catch if he could have his own way, and moved away; and Frank was left to finish his dinner in peace.

That afternoon, a soldier, whose name was Cabot, came and sat down beside Frank, and inquired:

"Didn't you try to escape last night?"

"Yes, but I was discovered."

"You would not have been, if one of our own men hadn't split on you."

"What!" exclaimed Frank, "you don't pretend to say that a Federal soldier was mean enough to inform against me?"

"Yes, I do; and there he stands now." And, as Cabot spoke, he pointed to a tall, hard-featured man standing by the window, looking out into the street. "I slept at the head of the stairs last night, and distinctly heard him tell the guards that you were intending to leave. His name is Bishop, and he belongs to the Thirtieth Maine Regiment. He has for some time past been trying to be allowed to take the oath of allegiance to the South." [Footnote: A fact.]

"What will he do then?" inquired Frank; "go into the rebel army?"

"No, but he could be employed here in the arsenal, making bullets to kill our own men with."

"The scoundrel!" exclaimed Frank, indignantly; "I didn't suppose there was a man from my own State who could be guilty of such meanness."

"He is mean enough for any thing. Haven't you noticed that every night he comes around through our quarters with a candle?"

"Yes; but I don't know what he does it for."

"Well, he counts us every night before he goes to sleep, and, in fact, comes through our room two or three times in the night, to see that none of us have escaped. He hopes in that manner to gain favor with the rebels. I have told you this, in order that you may look out for him the next time you try to escape."

Frank was astounded at this intelligence, and, at first, he did not believe it. But that evening, about nine o'clock, Bishop came in, as usual, with his candle, and Frank inquired:

"What made you tell the guard that I was going to escape last night?"

The question was asked so suddenly - and in a manner which showed Bishop that Frank was well acquainted with his treachery - that he dared not deny the charge, and he answered:

"Because, when any of our boys escape, the guards are awful hard on those of us that are left."

"That's no excuse at all," answered Frank. "If you were a man, you would have endeavored to escape long ago, instead of staying here and trying to make friends with the enemies of your country. You're a black-hearted scoundrel and traitor! and I tell you, once for all, that if you ever come into my quarters again after dark, you'll never go out alive. We all know about your operations here."

Bishop made no reply, but turned to walk on, when Frank rose to his feet, and exclaimed:

"Hold on, here! you are not going through this room with that candle. Go back instantly where you belong, and don't show your face in here again."

Bishop saw that Frank was in earnest, and, without saying a word, he turned and walked into his quarters.

Frank had a twofold object in talking to him as he did. He wanted to let him know that his fellow-prisoners all knew what he had done, and he wished, also, to deter him from coming into that room again, as he had determined to make another attempt at escape that very night. The traitor had no sooner disappeared than Frank descended the stairs that led down into the hall, at the foot of which there were two guards posted.

"Hallo, Yank!" said one of them, as Frank came down, "I reckon as how you had better travel right back up sta'rs agin, 'cause it's agin orders to 'low you fellers to come down here a'ter dark."

"I know it is," answered Frank; "but it is so awful hot up stairs that I can't stand it. You'll let me stay down here long enough to cool off a little, won't you?"

"Wal," answered the guard, who really seemed to be a kind-hearted fellow, "I reckon as how you mought stay here a minit; but you mustn't stay no longer."

"All right," answered Frank; and he seated himself on the lower step, and talked with the guards until he was informed that it was high time he was "travelin' back up sta'rs."

"Very well," answered Frank, rising to his feet, and stretching himself, "I'll go, if you want me to."

And he *did* go. With one bound he dashed by the astonished

guards, and, before they could fire a shot, he had disappeared in the darkness.

His escape had been accomplished much easier than he had anticipated. He had expected at least a shot from the guards, and, perhaps, a struggle with them; for, when he left his quarters, he had determined to escape, or die in the attempt. In a few moments he reached the bushes that lined the road on both sides, and threw himself flat among them, and determined to wait until his pursuers had passed on, so that he would be on their trail, instead of having them on his. It was well that he had adopted this precaution, for he had scarcely concealed himself before the roll of a drum announced that the guards were being aroused, and that the pursuit was about to commence; and presently a squad of cavalry dashed rapidly by, and a crashing in the bushes told him that a party of men were searching the woods for him. As soon as his pursuers were out of hearing, Frank rose to his feet, and ran along the road, close to the bushes, so that, if he heard any one approaching, he would have a place of concealment close at hand. He had made, perhaps, half a mile in this way, when he discovered a man pacing up and down the road, with a musket on his shoulder. He was evidently a picket; and Frank, knowing that his comrades were not far off, drew back into the bushes, out of sight. Which way should he go now? This was a question which he could not answer satisfactorily. There was, doubtless, another picket-post not far off, and if, in going through the woods, he should stumble upon it, he would be shot down before he had a chance for flight. Should he attempt to pass the sentinel by strategy? This seemed to be the most feasible plan, for he would have a much better chance to escape in running by one man, than risking the shots of half a dozen. Besides, he had no weapon whatever, and he resolved to secure the picket's gun, if possible; so, waiting until his back was turned, he came out of his place of concealment, and approached him.

"Who comes there?" shouted the picket.

"A friend," answered Frank.

"Advance, friend, and give the countersign."

"Never mind the countersign," answered Frank; "I haven't got it. Have you seen any thing of an escaped Yankee prisoner out here?"

"No," answered the rebel, lowering his gun, which he had held at a charge bayonet. "He didn't come around here. But a company of cavalry went by just now, and my relief went with them."

"And left you here alone?" said Frank, who had continued to approach the picket, until he was now within arm's length of him.

"Yes," answered the rebel; "and I think it is a pretty way to do business, for it is time I was" -

He never finished the sentence; for Frank sprang upon him like a tiger, and seizing his throat, with a powerful gripe, threw him to the ground; and, hastily catching up the musket which had fallen from his enemy's hand, dealt him a severe blow on the head. The muscles of the rebel instantly relaxed; and Frank - after unbuckling his cartridge-box, and fastening it to his own waist - shouldered his musket, and ran boldly along the road. He traveled until almost daylight, without seeing any one, and then turned off into the woods.

About noon, he came to a road, and, as he was crossing it, a bullet whistled past him, and, the next moment, a party of rebels, whom he had not noticed, dashed down the road in pursuit. Frank returned the shot, and then started for the woods, loading his musket as he went. He soon had the satisfaction of seeing that he was gaining on his pursuers, and, although the bullets whizzed by his head in unpleasant proximity, he escaped unhurt. The rebels, however, were not so fortunate; for Frank fired as fast as he could load his gun, and at every shot a rebel measured his length on the ground.

For almost two hours his pursuers remained within gun-shot; but finding it impossible to capture him, or, perhaps, struck with terror at his skill as a marksman, they abandoned the pursuit. This was a lucky circumstance for Frank, for, to his astonishment and terror, he discovered that his last cartridge had been expended. But still, he was rejoicing over his escape, when a man rose out of the bushes, close at his side, and seized him by the collar.

# CHAPTER XIII

## THE FAITHFUL NEGRO

"Wal, now, I'll be dog-gone, but you are lively on your legs, for a little one," exclaimed the rebel, with a laugh. "But you're a safe Yank now."

"Not yet, I ain't," answered Frank. "I want you to understand that it's my principle never to surrender without a fight;" and, suddenly exerting all his strength, he tore himself away from his captor, leaving part of his collar in his grasp.

The rebel was taken completely by surprise, for he had supposed that Frank would surrender without a struggle; but the latter brought his musket to a charge bayonet, in a way that showed he was in earnest. The rebel was the better armed, carrying a neat sporting rifle, to which was attached a long, sharp saber-bayonet. Frank noticed this difference, but resolutely stood his ground, and, as he was very expert in the bayonet exercise, and as his enemy appeared to be but very little his superior in strength and agility, he had no fear as to the result of the conflict.

At length the rebel, after eyeing his youthful antagonist for a moment, commenced maneuvering slowly, intending, if possible, to draw him out. But Frank stood entirely on the defensive; failing in this mode of attack, the rebel began to grow excited, and became quicker in his movements. But his efforts were useless, for Frank - although a little pale, which showed that he knew the struggle must end in the death of one or the other of them - did not retreat an inch, but coolly parried every thrust made by his infuriated enemy, with the skill of a veteran. The rebel was again obliged to change his plan of attack, and commenced by rushing furiously upon Frank, endeavoring to beat down his guard by mere strength. But this proved his ruin; for Frank met him promptly at all points, and, watching the moment when the rebel carelessly opened his guard, he sprang forward and buried his bayonet to the hilt in his breast. The thrust was mortal, and the rebel threw his arms above his head, and sank to the ground without a groan.

"I believe he's done for," said Frank to himself; and he stepped up to take a nearer look at his enemy. There he lay, his pale face upturned, and the blood running from an ugly wound in the region of his heart. "I do believe he *is* dead," repeated Frank, with a shudder, as he gazed sorrowfully at he work he had done. "But there was no alternative between his death and a long confinement in prison. It was done in self-defense;" and he turned to walk away.

Just then the thought struck him that he would take the rebel's gun; his own was worse than useless, for his cartridges had all been expended. So, throwing down his heavy musket, he picked up the rifle his enemy had carried, and, slinging the powder-horn and bullet-pouch over his shoulder, he started off through the woods.

But where should he go? His escape, and the manner in which it was accomplished, had doubtless aroused the entire country. The woods around him were filled with rebels, and the question was, in which direction should he turn to avoid them? After some hesitation, he determined to go as directly through the woods, toward the river, as possible, and, if discovered, trust to his woodcraft and swiftness of foot to save him. With this determination, he shouldered his rifle and walked rapidly on, taking care, however, to keep a good look-out on all sides, and to make as little noise as possible. All sounds of the pursuit had died away, and the woods were as silent as midnight. But even this was a source of fear to Frank; for he knew not what tree or thicket concealed an enemy, nor how soon the stillness would be broken by the crack of a rifle and the whistle of a hostile bullet.

At length the sun went down, and it began to grow dark; but still Frank walked on, wishing to get as far away from the scene of the fight as possible. Presently he heard a sound that startled him: it was the clatter of horses' hoofs, on a hard, well-beaten road. Nearer and nearer came the sound, and, in a few moments, a company of cavalry passed by, and Frank could distinctly hear them laughing and talking with each other.

When they were out of hearing, he paused to deliberate. It was evident that he could not travel through those deep woods at night; should he wait until it became dark, and then boldly follow the road, or should he remain where he was until morning? There was one great objection to the first proposition, and that was his uniform, and the danger he would run of being captured by the night patrol, which he knew were stationed at intervals along the road. It did not seem possible for him to remain where he was; for now, that he had partly got over his excitement, he began to feel the cravings of hunger; in fact, it almost rendered him desperate, and he began to wish that he had surrendered without a struggle, or that he had not attempted to escape at all, for, if he were a prisoner, he could probably obtain sufficient food to keep him from starving. But he knew that his time was too precious to be wasted with such foolish thoughts; besides, when he thought of home and his mother, who had evidently heard of his capture, all ideas of surrendering himself vanished, and he felt that he could endure any thing, even starvation, if he only had the assurance that he would see home once more. But he knew that wishing would not bring him out of his present difficulty: he must work for his liberty; do every thing in his power, and leave the rest to Providence.

He started out again, and determined that his first step should be to reconnoiter the road. No one was in sight; but, about a quarter of a mile down the road, on the other side, was a large plantation-house, with its neat negro quarters clustering around it, and looking altogether like a little village. He knew that some of the cabins were inhabited, for he saw the smoke wreathing out of the chimneys; could he not go to one of them, and obtain food? He had often heard of escaped prisoners being fed and sheltered by the negroes; why could not he throw himself under their protection? He must have something to satisfy his hunger; and if he could but gain the woods on the opposite side of the road, it would require but a few moments to reach the house. He determined to try it. Glancing hastily up and down the road, he clutched his rifle desperately, and started. A few rapid steps carried him across the road; he cleared the fence at a bound, and was out of sight, in the bushes, in a moment. He immediately started for the nearest cabin and, in a few moments, came to a stand-still in a thicket of bushes just behind it. There was some one in the cabin, for he could see a light shining through the cracks between the logs; and he distinctly heard the music of a violin, and a voice singing:

"The sun shines bright in my ole Kentucky home" -

But still he hesitated to advance; his courage had failed him. What, if the negro - for he was certain it was a negro in the cabin – should betray him? What if - His reverie was suddenly interrupted by the approach of a horseman on the road. Presently a rebel officer rode leisurely by. When he arrived opposite the house, a man, who was sitting on the portico, and whom Frank had not noticed, hailed the horseman, who drew in his rein, and stopped.

"Have you caught them all yet?" inquired the man on the portico.

"No," answered the officer; "not yet. One of them gave us the slip; a little fellow; belongs to the gun-boats. He's around here somewhere; but we'll have him to-morrow, for he can't escape.

If he comes around here, and you think there is any chance to take him alive, just send down to the Forks for us. If not, you had better shoot him. I wouldn't advise you to meddle with him much, however, for he's a dead shot, and fights like a cuss."

"Did he kill any of the boys?" asked the man on the portico.

"Yes; he killed Bill Richards, who was on guard at the time he escaped, and stole his musket and cartridge-box. I suppose you heard of that. And then, when we got after him, he ran through the woods like a deer, loading his gun as he went, and every time he turned around, somebody had to drop. Finally, old Squire Davis's son overtook him, and they had a regular hand-to-hand fight; but the little one, as usual, came out at the top of the heap."

"Did he kill young Davis?"

"Yes, as dead as a smelt; stuck a bayonet clean through his heart. But I must be going. Keep an eye out for him!"

"All right," answered the man on the portico; and the horseman rode off.

What Frank's feelings were, as he lay there in the bushes, and listened to this conversation - every word of which he overheard - we will not attempt to say. But it showed him that his enemies feared him, and dreaded to meet him single-handed; and that, if he were retaken, his life would not be worth a moment's purchase. He had all along been perfectly aware that his case was desperate, and that he had undertaken something at which many a person, with twice his years and experience, would have hesitated. His condition seemed utterly hopeless. He had never before realized his danger, or what would be his fate if he were captured; but now all the difficulties before him seemed to stand out in bold relief. Yet this knowledge did not act upon him as with some persons; it only nerved him for yet greater exertions, and with a determination to brave every danger before him.

When the horseman had disappeared, and the man on the portico had returned to his seat, Frank again turned his attention to the cabin. After putting a new cap on his rifle, he threw it into the hollow of his arm, and crawled noiselessly out of his place of concealment. When he reached the cabin, he raised to his feet, boldly ascended the steps, and knocked at the door, intending, if his demand for food was not instantly complied with, to take it by force.

"Who dar?" inquired a voice from the inside.

Frank made no reply, but was about to repeat the summons, when the door was thrown open, and an old, gray-headed negro woman appeared before him. Frank was about to make known his wants, when the woman, who had thrown the door wide open, to allow the light to fall upon him, exclaimed:

"Why, de Lor' A'mighty bress us! Come in, chile. What is you standin' out dar for? Come in, I tol' you." And Frank was seized by the arm and pulled into the cabin, and the door was closed carefully behind him.

"Stop dat 'ar fiddlin', ole man," continued the woman, addressing herself to an aged negro, who was seated in an easy chair in the chimney corner; "stop dat 'ar fiddlin', an' git up an' give young massa dat cheer."

"I don't wish to give you any trouble," said Frank. "I'm not the least bit tired; but I would like something to eat."

"No trouble 't all, chile," said the old woman. "Now, don't you go talkin' 'bout trouble, I knows who you is. Set down dar." And the old woman pointed to the chair which the man had vacated. "I'll give you somethin' to eat, right away. Pomp, ole man, git up an' cut some o' dat ham;" and the woman bustled about in a state of considerable excitement.

Frank hid his rifle behind a coat which hung in one corner of the cabin, and was about to take possession of the chair, when hasty steps were heard on the walk leading to the cabin.

"Gorry mighty!" exclaimed the old negro, in alarm, "dar come de oberseer. Git under the bed - quick, young massa. You'll be safe dar - quick."

Frank had hardly time to act upon this suggestion, when the door suddenly opened, and a shaggy head appeared.

"Haven't you had your supper yet, Pomp, you black rascal?" inquired the overseer, witnessing the preparations for cooking that were going on.

"I's only been home a few minutes, massa," answered Pomp.

"Well, hurry up, then. I came here," continued the overseer, "to tell you that there is a Yankee prowling around here somewhere; if he comes here, I want you to send for me. Do you understand?"

"Yes, massa," answered Pomp.

"Don't you feed him, or do any thing else for him," continued the overseer. "If you do, I'll whip you to death. Now, mind what I tell you." And the overseer closed the door, and departed, to carry the same information and warning to the other cabins.

As soon as the sound of his footsteps had died away, Pomp whispered:

"All right now, young massa. You can come out now - no danger. The oberseer won't come to dis house g'in dis night."

Frank, accordingly, crawled out from under the bed, and seated himself in the easy chair, while the old woman went on with her cooking. In a few minutes, which seemed an age to

Frank, however, the meal, which consisted of coffee, made of parched corn, ham, honey, and corn-bread, was ready. Frank thought he had never eaten so good a meal before. He forgot the danger of his situation, and listened to the conversation of the old negro and his wife, as though there was not a rebel within a hundred miles of him.

"There," he exclaimed, after he had finished the last piece of corn-bread, and pushed his chair back from the table, "I believe I've eaten supper enough to satisfy any two men living."

"Has yer had enough, chile?" asked the old woman. "I's glad to see yer eat. I wants to do all I can for you Yankee sogers."

"Oh, I've had a great plenty, aunty," answered Frank, as he rose from the table. "Now, I must bid you good-by," he continued, as he pulled his rifle out from its hiding-place. "I shall never be able to repay you; but" -

"Lor' A'mighty, chile!" interrupted the old woman, "whar's you gwine? You mustn't say one word 'bout gwine out o' dis house *dis* night. I's got a bed all fixed for you, an' Pomp will take you up early in de mornin', an' show you de way fru de swamp."

"Put away dat gun, young massa," chimed in Pomp; "dere's no danger."

Frank could not resist this appeal, for the bed, which the old woman had made for him in one corner of the cabin, rough as it was, was a pleasant sight to his eyes. So, after hiding his rifle under one of the quilts, where he could get his hand upon it at a moment's warning, he threw himself upon the bed without removing his clothes, and was fast asleep in a moment. It seemed to him that he had hardly closed his eyes, when a hand was laid on his shoulder, and Pomp's voice whispered in his ear:

"Wake up, young massa; 'most daylight."

"You sleep mighty sound, chile," said the old woman, as Frank rose from the bed. "I's sorry to be 'bilged to 'sturb you, but you must be gwine now. Here's a little bite for you to eat." As she spoke, she handed Frank a haversack, such as he had often seen used by the soldiers of the rebel army, filled with corn-bread and cold ham. Frank slung it over his shoulder, and, after pulling his rifle out from under the bed, said:

"Aunty, I thank you for your kindness to" -

"Lor' A'mighty, chile!" interrupted the woman, "don't say one word 'bout dat, I tol' you. I's sorry we can't do more for you; but you must go away now. May de good Lor' bress you."

The tears rolled down the old woman's cheeks as she said this, and Frank silently shook her hand, and followed Pomp out into the darkness.

# CHAPTER XIV

## CHASED BY BLOOD-HOUNDS

The moon had gone down, the stars were hidden by thick, heavy clouds, and it was so dark that it was impossible to distinguish the nearest objects. Every thing was as silent as death; but this did not affect the vigilance of Pomp, who led the way with noiseless steps, pausing, now and then, to listen. They met with no difficulty, however, and, in a few moments, the plantation was left behind, and they entered the swamp. It was a chilly, gloomy place, and the darkness was impenetrable; but Frank relied implicitly on his guide, who seemed to understand what he was about, and kept as close behind him as possible.

For an hour they traveled without speaking; at length Pomp stopped on the bank of a narrow but deep stream.

"Can you swim, young massa?" he inquired, turning to Frank.

"Yes, like a duck," was the reply.

"I's mighty glad to h'ar it," said Pomp, "'cause den you're safe. But I's been mighty oneasy 'bout it, 'cause, if you can't swim, you're kotched, shore. Now," he continued, "I must leave you here, 'cause I don't want to let any one know dat I's been away from de plantation. You must cross dis creek, and foller dat road," pointing to a narrow, well-beaten bridle-path on the opposite bank, "an' dat will lead you straight to de Red Ribber.

You must keep a good watch, now, 'cause you'll h'ar something 'fore long dat'll make you wish you had nebber been born. I's heered it often, an' I knows what it is. Good-by; an' de Lor' bress an' protect you;" and, before Frank could speak, Pomp had disappeared.

Alone! The young hero had never before comprehended the full meaning of that single word, as he did now. Alone, in an almost unbroken forest, which was filled with enemies, who were thirsting for his blood; with no one to whom he could go for advice or assistance. Is it to be wondered that he felt lonely and discouraged?

He looked back to the scenes through which he had passed: the fight; his capture; the long, weary march, under a burning sun; his treatment in the prison, the escape, and the pursuit; the hand-to-hand struggle in the woods; all came up vividly before him, and he wondered how he had escaped unhurt; and, then, what had the future in store for him? The warning of the faithful Pomp was still ringing in his ears, and a dread of impending evil, which he could not shake off, continually pressed upon him. For the first time since his escape, Frank was completely unnerved. Seating himself on the ground, he covered his face with his hands, and cried like a child.

But this burst of weakness did not continue long, for he did not forget that he was still in danger. Hastily dashing the tears from his eyes, he rose to his feet, and prepared to cross the stream. Holding his rifle and ammunition above his head with one hand, he swam with the other, reached the opposite bank in safety, and followed the path into the swamp. A mile further on, he came to another stream, and was making preparations to cross it, when he was startled by a voice, which sounded from the opposite bank:

"Who goesh dere?"

Instead of replying to the challenge, Frank sprang behind a tree, and, looking across the stream, discovered a tall, powerfully-built man, dressed in "butternut" clothes, holding his rifle in the hollow of his arm. In an instant Frank's gun was at his shoulder, and his finger was already pressing the trigger, when the man exclaimed:

"What for you shoot? I be a friend."

Frank, although fearful of treachery, lowered his gun, and the Dutchman, moving out of the bushes, leaned on his rifle, and inquired:

"Where you go? I guess you been a gun-boat feller; ain't it?"

"Yes," answered Frank, "I once belonged to a gun-boat. But who are you?"

"Me? Oh, I was a captain in the army. Sherman gets licked at Wicksburg, an' I gets took brisoner; an' purty quick me an' anoder feller runs away. Here he is;" and, as the Dutchman spoke, a man wearing a shabby Confederate uniform appeared.

Frank's mind was made up in an instant. Beyond a doubt this was but a stratagem to capture him. But he resolved that he would never surrender, as long as he had sufficient strength to handle his rifle.

"Well, my young friend," exclaimed the man in the rebel uniform, "this is a nice dress for a Federal officer to be wearing, isn't it?"

"I don't believe that either of you are officers in the Federal army," answered Frank. "It's my opinion that you are both rebels. If it is your intention to attempt to capture me, I may as well tell you that your expectations will never be realized, for I shall never be taken alive;" and Frank handled the lock of his gun in a very significant manner.

"I admire your grit," said the man, "and I acknowledge that you have strong grounds for suspicion. But we are really escaped prisoners."

"Yah," chimed in the Dutchman, "I shwear dat is so."

"It is no fault of ours," continued the man, "that we are wearing rebel uniforms; for we were compelled to exchange with our captors, and were obliged to accept these, or go without any."

"What regiment do you belong to?"

"The One Hundred and Twenty-ninth Illinois Infantry, Company 'K.' I formerly belonged to the Forty-sixth Maine."

"Do you know any of the boys belonging to Company 'B,' of the Forty-sixth Maine Regiment?"

"Oh, yes," replied the man, "I know Harry and George Butler, Ben Lake, and, in fact, all the boys; for I once belonged to that very company. My home is only twenty miles from Lawrence, the place where the company was raised."

Frank did not stop to ask any more questions, for he was satisfied that he had fallen in with friends. How his heart bounded at meeting one who had lived so near his own home! He hastily crossed the stream, and, seizing the man's hand, shook it heartily.

"I am overjoyed at meeting with you, sir," he said, in a voice choked with emotion. "Perhaps I owe you an apology; but you will acknowledge that it is best to be on the safe side."

"Certainly it is," answered the man. "I should have done exactly as you did, if I had been in your place. But where are you travelling to?"

"I want to reach Red River, as soon as possible."

"So do we! But we have lost our reckoning, and don't know

which way to go."

"I do," said Frank. "This path leads directly to it."

They did not linger long to converse - time was too precious for that - but immediately struck into the path, Frank leading the way. He soon learned that the names of his newly-found friends were Major Williams and Captain Schmidt. They had been captured, with two hundred others, at the battle of Vicksburg, and had escaped while being taken into Texas. They had accomplished, perhaps, half a dozen miles from the place where they met, when the breeze bore to their ears a sound that made Frank turn as pale as death, and tremble as though suddenly seized with a fit of the ague. They all heard it; but he was the only one who knew what it was.

"What ish dat, ony how?" coolly inquired the captain.

Before Frank could reply, the fearful sound was repeated, faint and far off, but still nearer than before.

"Merciful heavens!" ejaculated the major, who now understood their situation; "is it possible you don't know what that sound is? *It is the cry of a blood-hound!*"

"Oh, yah!" exclaimed the captain, as though the idea had suddenly come into his head, "I did think it vas a dorg."

"Push ahead now, boys, for Heaven's sake!" exclaimed the major. "Push ahead as fast as possible."

The captain evidently did not comprehend the danger of their situation; but Frank and the major knew that their lives depended upon the next few moments. Oh, how thankful was Frank that he was not alone! He now knew the meaning of Pomp's warning; and the dreadful sound had so unnerved him, that it was with great difficulty he could keep on his way. But this lasted only for a moment. His fear changed to indignation, and a desire to execute vengeance on men who could be guilty of such barbarity. It seemed as though the strength of a dozen men was suddenly infused into him; so, shouldering his rifle, he ran along the path with a speed that made it difficult for the Dutchman to keep pace with him. But, fast as they went, the fearful sound grew louder and louder; and, finally, they distinctly heard the clatter of horses' hoofs, and voices cheering on the dogs.

"Hurry on, for mercy's sake," said the major.

"Mine Gott in Himmel!" ejaculated the captain, who was puffing and blowing like a porpoise; "I can't run no faster. I guess it's petter we stops and fights 'em, ain't it? I been not a good feller to run!"

"You *must* run a little further," said Frank. "We will certainly be captured, if we stop to fight them here."

The captain made no reply, but kept along as close behind the major as possible. Frank's swiftness of foot was standing him well in hand now, for he frequently found himself obliged to slacken his pace, in order to allow his friends to come up with him. But his usual confidence was gone. He knew he could not stand that rapid pace much longer. Soon they must stop and fight; and what if the dogs, which would, undoubtedly, be some distance in advance of the horsemen, should overpower them? Frank had often read of the ferocity of these blood-hounds, and the thought of being pulled down and torn to pieces by them in those dark woods, and the knowledge that his mother and sister would forever remain ignorant of his fate, was terrible. Suddenly, an abrupt bend in the path brought them to the banks of another of those narrow streams with which the country was intersected like a net-work. What a cheering sight it was to Frank's eyes! He now saw some chance for escape; and, without hesitating a moment, he plunged into the water. The others were close at his heels, and a few bold strokes brought them to the opposite shore.

"Here we are," said the major. "Our chance for escape is rather

Harry Castlemon

slim, but we will make a stand here."

They had scarcely concealed themselves in the bushes, when one of the hounds appeared on the bank. He was followed by another, and still another, until eight of the terrible animals were in sight. They followed the trail of the fugitives down to the edge of the water, where, finding themselves at fault, they separated, and commenced beating up and down the bank, now and then looking toward the opposite shore, and uttering their bays, which sounded in Frank's ears like the knell of death.

"I pelieve I shoots one of them dorgs, ain't it?" said the captain; and he thrust his rifle cautiously through the bushes.

"No, no," commanded the major, "save your ammunition. The men will be here in a minute. Here they come now." And, as he spoke, there was a loud crashing in the bushes, and four horsemen came in sight.

"Thunder!" exclaimed one of them, who wore the uniform of a colonel, "I was in hopes we should catch the rascal before he reached this place. Here, Tige," he continued, addressing a powerful white hound, "hunt 'em up, hunt 'em up!"

The hound ran down to the edge of the stream, and barked and whined furiously, but still hesitated to enter; for hounds are always averse to going into water.

"Hunt 'em up, sir!" shouted the colonel, angrily.

The dog, evidently, feared his master more than the water, for he plunged in, and commenced swimming toward the place where Frank and his companions were concealed; and the others, after a little hesitation, followed him.

"Ready, now, boys," whispered the major. "Captain, you shoot that white hound. Frank, you take the colonel, and I'll attend to the man just behind him. Don't waste your lead now."

The three rifles cracked in rapid succession, and the colonel and one of his men fell heavily from their saddles. The white hound gave one short howl of pain, and sank out of sight. Every shot had reached its mark.

The remaining rebels stood aghast at this sudden repulse; and the smoke of the rifles had scarcely cleared away, when they wheeled their horses, and disappeared in the woods.

The death of the white hound produced no less consternation among his canine assistants, for they each gave a short yelp, and turned and made for the shore.

# CHAPTER XV

## THE RESCUE

"Now's our time, boys," exclaimed the major; "come on, and load your guns as you run;" and he started rapidly down the path.

All sounds of the rebels were soon left behind; but our party kept on their way, until they emerged from the woods, and found themselves in full view of a plantation.

"I pelieve somebody lives in that house," exclaimed the captain, drawing back in the bushes.

"No doubt of it," answered the major.

"Let's move back into the woods a little further, and eat some dinner," said Frank; and he turned to walk away, and felt for the haversack the negro woman had given him. But it seemed that he was destined to disappointment, for the haversack was gone.

During all the perils he had encountered that day, he had been buoyed up by the thought that he had food sufficient to last him for a day or two, and that he was in no danger of suffering the pangs of hunger. But now his spirits fell again to zero.

"How unfortunate!" he exclaimed. "But it's just my luck."

"Yes, it is too bad," said the major; "for now we shall be obliged to run the risk of being captured, in order to procure food. But let us move on, and get as far away from this place as possible."

Frank silently shouldered his rifle, and followed the major, who threaded his way along in the edge of the woods, taking care to keep out of sight of any one who might be in the house. They kept on until dark, and then halted in the rear of another plantation, to hold a consultation relative to the manner in which they should obtain food.

"Well," said the major, "we must have something to eat, that's certain; and the only way I can think of, is to draw lots to see who shall go up to the house after it. It is a dangerous undertaking, but that is the fairest way to see who shall run the risk;" and the major selected three sticks of different lengths, and continued, as he held them out to Frank, in his closed hand, "Now, the one that draws the shortest stick must go to the house and procure us some food."

Frank drew first, then the captain, and the major took the one that was left. The lot fell upon Frank.

"Now," said the major, as he shook Frank's hand, "be careful of yourself, my friend. We will remain here until you return. When you get into the woods give two low whistles, that we may know that it is you. Good-by."

Frank silently returned the pressure of the major's hand, and moved away. He climbed over the fence that ran between the woods and the plantation, and walked fearlessly toward the house. He was not at all pleased with the part he had to perform, for he remembered the danger he had run the night before; but his determination was to do his duty, and trust to his skill to carry him safely through.

He shaped his course toward the negro quarters, which were in the rear of the house; but he soon discovered that these were entirely deserted. He carefully examined all the cabins, in hopes of finding a hen-roost, but in vain. His only alternative was to try the house. There was a light shining in the window, and Frank determined to reconnoiter the premises, and, if possible, learn who were in the house, before asking admittance. With this intention he shouldered his rifle, and was about to move forward, when he was startled by the sound of horses' hoofs behind him, and a voice exclaimed:

"Hullo, my friend! Have you an extra bed in the house, for a soldier?"

Frank turned, and found that the horseman was so close to him that flight was impossible. His first impulse was to shoot him where he sat; but he was still ignorant of the number of persons there might be in the house. Perhaps it was filled with soldiers. The report of his gun would certainly alarm them, and might lead to his capture. Besides, the man had addressed him as though he were the proprietor of the plantation; perhaps he might be able to obtain some information. So he answered, with some hesitation:

"Yes, I suppose there is an extra bed in the house; but I should really like to know who and what you are, before I agree to accommodate you."

"I am Lieutenant Somers," answered the rebel; "and I belong to the Seventeenth Georgia Infantry. You belong to the army too, do you not?" he continued, noticing the brass buttons on Frank's coat.

It was a lucky circumstance for the young hero that the night was so dark, or he would certainly have been discovered.

"Yes," he answered, in reply to the rebel's question, "I am in the service. But what are you doing around here this time of night?"

"I have been hunting after an escaped Yankee prisoner - a

gun-boat officer."

"Did you catch him?" inquired Frank.

"No; but I caught two others. I chased this gun-boat fellow with blood-hounds; but when I overtook him, I found that he had been reinforced by half a dozen others, and I was obliged to retreat. The scoundrels killed Colonel Acklen and one of his men, and the best blood-hound in Louisiana."

"Where are the prisoners you captured?" inquired Frank, hardly able to suppress his exultation at finding himself face to face with one of the men who had hunted him with blood-hounds.

"Oh, I left them at the back of the plantation, one of my men is keeping guard over them; but there is scarcely any need of that, for the Yankees are securely bound."

"They are, eh!" exclaimed Frank, who could restrain himself no longer. "Well, here is a Yankee who is not bound, and never intends to be;" and he raised his rifle to his shoulder, and glanced along the clean, brown barrel. "I am the gun-boat fellow you were pursuing with blood-hounds. So, if you wish to live five minutes longer, don't attempt to make any resistance."

The rebel was taken so completely by surprise that he could not utter a word, but sat on his horse as motionless and dumb as though he had been suddenly turned into a statue.

"Come down off that horse!" commanded his captor.

The rebel obeyed, without hesitation.

"Now, have you got any dangerous weapons about you?" inquired Frank. "Tell the truth, now, for your life isn't worth a picayune."

"Yes," answered the rebel, "I have a revolver and a Bowie-knife;" and he raised his hand to his breast pocket.

"Hands down! hands down!" exclaimed Frank; "I want to examine your pockets myself;" and he stepped forward and relieved the rebel of a Bowie-knife, a revolver, several cartridges, a flint and steel, and some papers. These, with the exception of the revolver, he laid carefully on the ground, and placed his rifle beside them. "Now," continued Frank, "it would be a great accommodation if you would trade uniforms with me. The people in this part of the country don't seem to like Uncle Sam's clothes very well. Come out of that coat."

The rebel hesitated to obey.

"Come out of that coat, Lieutenant Somers," repeated Frank, slowly; and he raised his revolver until it was on a line with his captive's head.

The sight of his own weapon, whose qualities he probably knew full well, brought the rebel to his senses, and he quickly divested himself of his coat.

"Now, pull off those pants," commanded his captor.

The rebel obeyed; and Frank continued, as he divested himself of his own clothes: "Now, if you wish, you can put on these."

The rebel had no other alternative, and he slowly donned the naval uniform, while Frank quickly converted himself into a fine-looking rebel lieutenant. He then carefully pocketed the articles which he had taken from the rebel, with the exception of the papers.

"What are these?" he inquired.

"The one in the brown envelope is my appointment, and the others are orders to take my company and act as scouts."

The latter were just what Frank wanted.

"Now," said Frank, going up to the horse, which had stood patiently by, "I have one more favor to ask of you, you mean, sneaking rebel, and then I am done with you. I want you to show me where you left your prisoners. But, in the first place, I am going into that house to get something to eat."

"I hope to thunder that you will be gobbled up," said the lieutenant, angrily.

"Easy, easy!" exclaimed Frank; "you are talking treason when you wish evil to befall one of Uncle Sam's boys; and I am not one to stand by and listen to it; so keep a civil tongue in your head, or I shall be obliged to put a stopper on your jaw. As I said before," he continued, "I am going into that house to get some supper; and, as I wish you to remain here until I come back, I shall take the liberty to tie your hands and feet. That's the way you serve your prisoners, I believe."

As Frank spoke, he cut the bridle from the horse with his Bowie-knife, and securely bound the rebel - who submitted to the operation with a very bad grace - and laid him away, as he would a log of wood, behind one of the cabins.

"Now, you barbarian," he continued, as he shouldered his rifle, and thrust the revolver and Bowie-knife into his belt, "you are in the power of one who has very little love for a man who is guilty of the cruelty of hunting a fellow-being with blood-hounds; so, if you expect to live to see daylight, don't make any noise." With this piece of advice, Frank left his captive, and started for the house.

He walked up the steps that led to the portico, which ran entirely around the house, and boldly knocked at the door. The summons was answered by a fine-looking, elderly lady, who, as soon as she saw the Confederate uniform, exclaimed:

"Good evening, sir; walk in."

Frank followed the lady through the hall, into a large room, whose only inmates were three young ladies, who rose and bowed as he came in. He was very much relieved to find that there were no men in the house.

"Take a chair, sir," said the elderly lady. "Is there any thing we can do for you?"

"Yes, ma'am," answered Frank. "I am out on a scout with some of my men, and my provisions have given out. I have taken the liberty to come here and see if I could not purchase some from you."

"We are glad to see you," said one of the young ladies. "I will have some food put up for you immediately; and you shall have a nice, warm supper before you go."

"I am under obligations to you, madam," answered Frank; "but, really, I can not wait, for I am on the trail of some escaped Yankee prisoners; and, besides, I always make it a point never to fare better than the men I command."

"I should like to have you stay," said the elderly lady, whom Frank set down as the mother of the girls; "but you know your duty better than we do. I wish all of our officers were as careful of their men, and as devoted to the cause, as you are. But what regiment do you belong to?"

"The Seventeenth Georgia," answered Frank.

"Did you catch any of the Yankees you are after?"

"No, ma'am, not yet. But we shall have them before to-morrow night."

"Oh, I hope so! I suppose you will hang them to the nearest tree, as fast as you catch them?"

"No, ma'am, I can't do that. They will be prisoners, you know, and must be treated as such."

"Then bring them here, and I will hang them for you," exclaimed the lady, excitedly. "I think our government is entirely too lenient with the rascals."

During the conversation that followed, Frank gained some very valuable information concerning the plans the rebels had on foot for the capture of the runaways. He also learned that the lady's husband was an officer of high rank in the rebel army, and that she was expecting him home every moment. Frank, as may be supposed, was not very well pleased with this information, and he cast uneasy glances toward the door, expecting to see the officer enter. But his fears were soon set at rest by the return of the young lady from the kitchen, with a large traveling bag, filled with provisions.

When Frank inquired what was to pay, he was informed that any one who would think of charging a soldier for provisions ought to be tarred and feathered and sent into the Yankee lines. This was good news to Frank, for, if there had been any thing to pay, he would not have known how to act, as money was a thing he had not seen for many a day. So, after thanking the ladies for their kindness, and bidding them good-night, he picked up his provisions and started out.

"Now, you man that hunts Union soldiers with blood-hounds," he exclaimed, as he walked up to his captive, and untied the strap with which his feet were bound, "get up, and lead me to the place where you left your prisoners;" and Frank seized the rebel by the collar, and helped him rather roughly to his feet.

The rebel made no reply, but led the way down the road which ran through the plantation. Frank followed close behind him, carrying his rifle and provisions in one hand, and his revolver in the other. At length they came to the fence at the end of the field, and, as he was helping his prisoner over, a voice from the woods called out:

"Who goes there?"

"Is that your man?" inquired Frank, in a whisper, turning to his prisoner.

"Yes," answered the rebel, gruffly.

"Then keep your mouth shut, and let me talk to him," commanded Frank. Raising his voice, he answered to the hail, "Friend!"

"Is that you, Lieutenant Somers?" inquired the voice.

"Yes," answered Frank. "Come here; I've got a supply of provisions, and another prisoner."

"Another Yank, eh!" said the man; and Frank heard him coming through the woods toward him.

"Well, we've one less to catch, then. Where is he? Let's have a squint at him."

"Never mind the prisoner," exclaimed Frank, "but come and take these provisions; they're heavy."

The rebel, who could not discover that any thing was wrong, reached out his hand, and took the traveling-bag from Frank, when the latter suddenly seized him by the collar, and exclaimed, as he pressed the muzzle of his revolver against his head:

"You're my prisoner!"

For an instant the rebel appeared utterly dumfounded; then, suddenly recovering himself, he struck up Frank's arm, and, with a quick movement, tore himself away from his grasp, and drew his Bowie-knife.

"Kill him, Jake! Kill him!" shouted the lieutenant, who, of

course, was unable to assist his man, as his hands were securely bound behind his back.

But Frank was too quick for him, for, before the rebel could make a thrust with his knife, the sharp report of the revolver echoed through the woods, and the man sank to the ground like a log.

"Now," exclaimed Frank, turning to his prisoner, "I've a good notion to shoot you, also. But I will try you once more; and I tell you now, once for all, don't open your head again to-night, unless you are spoken to. Now, show me where you left your prisoners."

"Here we are!" exclaimed a voice from the bushes.

Frank soon found them, and, when he had cut the ropes with which they were bound, and set them at liberty, they each seized his hands, and wrung them in silent gratitude.

"Thank heaven, we're free men once more!" exclaimed one of the poor fellows. "But where is that lieutenant that captured us?"

"He's my prisoner," answered Frank.

"Here you are, you thunderin', low-lived secesh!" exclaimed the man, who had not yet spoken, as he walked up to the rebel, and laid his hand on his shoulder. "I've a mind to stop your wind for you, you mean" -

"Easy, easy, boys," exclaimed Frank; "he's a prisoner, you know, and we've no right to put him in misery simply because he's in our power."

"Why, the varmint hunted us yesterday with blood-hounds," exclaimed one of the soldiers.

"He served me the same way to-day," answered Frank; "but,

still, we have no right to abuse him. But I have two more friends around here somewhere;" and Frank put his hand to his mouth, and gave two low whistles. It was answered immediately, and a voice, which Frank recognized as the captain's, inquired:

"Ish dat you, you gun-boat feller?"

"Yes, I'm here, captain; come along."

The Dutchman soon made his appearance, followed by the major. They had remained in their hiding-place, and heard all that was going on; but, so fearful were they of treachery, that they dared not come out. Frank briefly related to them the circumstances connected with the capture of the lieutenant, and the release of the two soldiers; after this a consultation was held, and it was decided that it would not be prudent to attempt to reach Red River for a day or two, at least. The major thought it best to remain concealed during the day, and at night boldly follow the road.

This plan was adopted, for the entire party - including the soldiers Frank had just released - were dressed in butternut clothes; besides this, the papers which had been taken from the lieutenant would greatly assist them, if their plan was carried out with skill and determination. And, in regard to the prisoner - who, of course, had not heard a word of the consultation - it was decided to detain him for a day or two, in order that he might be led to believe that it was their intention to keep as far away from Red River as possible, and then release him.

After their plans had all been determined upon, Frank opened his sack of provisions, when, eating a scanty meal, they again started forward. They kept along on the edge of the plantations until the day began to dawn, and then turned into the woods and encamped.

# CHAPTER XVI

## A FRIEND IN NEED

In the evening, at dark, they resumed their journey. They boldly followed the road, and met with no opposition until just before daylight, when a voice directly in front of them shouted, "Halt!"

"Now, boys," whispered the major, "our safety depends upon our nerve. It is so dark they can't see our faces, so don't be frightened at any thing that may happen. Captain, take care of that prisoner, and remember and blow his brains out the moment he makes the least attempt at escape."

"Who goes there?" shouted the voice again.

"Scouts!" answered the major, promptly.

"Advance, one scout, and give the counter sign."

The Major accordingly advanced to the place where the sentry was standing, and the captain cautiously cocking his musket, placed its cold muzzle against the prisoner's head, whispering, between his clenched teeth:

"I guess you hear what the major did said, ain't it? Well, then, don't say somethings."

The laconic captain probably thought this warning sufficient, for he brought his musket to an "order arms," and did not afterward even deign to cast a single glance at the prisoner.

In the mean time, the major was endeavoring to convince the lieutenant of the guard that, although they did not have the countersign, they were in reality Confederate soldiers.

"It may be that you'uns is all right," said the lieutenant, after reading, by the aid of a dark lantern, the papers which Frank had captured. "But, you see, thar's so many of these yere Yanks running away, that we'uns has got to be mighty careful how we let folks go past."

"I tell you," said the major, speaking as though he considered himself highly insulted, "I tell you, that I am on special service by order of General Taylor. I have been out on a scout to recapture the very prisoners you have just mentioned. I have already caught one of them," he added, pointing to their prisoner, who, let it be remembered, was dressed in Frank's uniform.

"If you'uns is out on a scout," said a soldier, who had been aroused from his blanket, and pressed up to obtain a glance at the major, "whar's your hosses?"

"I left them about a mile down the river. I have already been through your lines once to-night, and I might have gone through this time without your knowledge, if I had seen fit to do so."

"Maybe it's all right," said the lieutenant, shaking his head dubiously; "but I'll be dog-gone if I don't think I've seen your face somewhere before;" and as he said this he raised the lantern, and allowed the light to shine full upon him. Frank, who had been waiting impatiently for the interview to be brought to a close, gave himself up for lost when he saw a smile of triumph light up the rebel's face. But the major was equal to the emergency. Meeting the lieutenant's gaze without flinching, he replied, carelessly:

"Very likely you have. I have been in the service ever since the war broke out. But do you intend to allow us to proceed, or shall I be obliged to report you at head-quarters? Remember, I can say that you do not keep a very good watch, seeing I have already passed you once."

This threat seemed to decide the lieutenant, who replied, "I guess it's all right - you'uns can pass."

When Frank heard this, it seemed as though a heavy load had been removed from his breast. But the hardest part of the trial, with him, had yet to come. What if he should be recognized? But he had that risk to run; so, summoning up all his fortitude, he marched with his companions by the guards, apparently as unconcerned as though he was entering a friendly camp.

The moment they got out of hearing of the tread of the sentinel, the major turned from the road and led the way into the woods. After walking a short distance, at a rapid pace, he whispered:

"Perhaps we fooled the rascals, but I think not. I didn't like the way that lieutenant eyed me. I am certain we shall be pursued as soon as he can send for assistance; and the best thing we can do is to get away from here. So, forward, double-quick. Don't make too much noise now. Captain, look out for that prisoner."

It was well that the major had adopted the precaution of leaving the road and taking to the woods, for, in less than half an hour after they had passed the guards, a squad of cavalry came up, having a full and correct description of Frank and his companions. By some means, the capture of the rebel lieutenant had become known, and a portion of his own regiment - which had followed Frank from Shreveport, but which had given up the chase and returned - had again started in pursuit. The guards were astounded when they learned that the young gun-boat officer (with whose flight and subsequent almost miraculous escapes from recapture every scout in the country was acquainted) had been within their very grasp, and a portion of them joined the cavalry in pursuit; but, as they kept on down the road, Frank and his companions again escaped. They had heard their pursuers pass by, and knowing that the country would be thoroughly alarmed, and that it would be useless to attempt to reach Red River at present, they directed their course toward Washita River, which lay about thirty-five miles distant, hoping to deceive the rebels as to their real intentions, and thus, by drawing their pursuers into the country, leave their avenue of escape unobstructed.

One clear, moonlight night they halted, as usual, in the rear of a plantation, and were debating upon the best means to be employed in obtaining food, when a man, dressed in a shabby Federal uniform, was discovered coming slowly toward them, on the opposite side of the fence that separated the woods from the plantation.

His sudden and wholly unexpected appearance took them completely by surprise. Frank immediately proposed to challenge him. Perhaps, like themselves, he was a fugitive from a rebel prison, and in need of assistance. But the captain strongly opposed this, and was in favor of shooting the man, who still continued to advance, as if wholly unconscious of the presence of any one - arguing, in his broken English, and with good reason, too, that the appearance of a Federal uniform in that part of the country boded them no good, but was a sure sign of treachery; and evidently thinking that he had won the day, he was about to put his plan into execution, when the major struck up his musket, and shouted:

"Who comes there?"

The stranger, instead of replying, instantly threw himself on the ground behind the fence, out of sight.

"Gott in himmel, major," exclaimed the disappointed captain, "I pelieve it's better you shoots that man - purty quick we all gets ketched again;" and as he said this the captain, who, although a very brave man on the field of battle, was very much opposed to fighting an invisible enemy, drew himself behind a tree, as if fully expecting to see a whole army of rebels rush out of their concealments upon them.

"Be quiet, captain," said the major. "You have grown very suspicious lately." Then, raising his voice, he called out: "Whoever you are behind that fence, whether a friend or an enemy to the Union, come out immediately, or you are a dead man."

A deep silence, which lasted for several seconds, followed his words. Then came the ominous click of half a dozen gun-locks, which, in the stillness of the night, could be heard a long distance.

The stranger evidently heard it too, for, without further hesitation, he arose from behind the fence, and came forward.

The major allowed him to approach within a few yards, and then ordered him to halt, and inquired:

"Now, sir! who and what are you? Tell the truth, for you have desperate men to deal with."

"From your language," answered the stranger, in a voice so soft that it was almost feminine, but which, nevertheless, betrayed not the slightest trepidation, "I should judge that you are escaped prisoners; if so, permit me to make one of your number. If not, you will find me as desperate as yourselves; for I have suffered too much in prison to ever allow myself to be taken back alive;" and, as he spoke, he displayed a brace of pistols, which showed that he meant what he said.

"Gott in himmel!" exclaimed the captain, springing out from behind his tree, and forgetting, in a moment, all his suspicions, "vos you captured, too? We been mighty glad to see you, any how."

"Yes," answered the man, "I have been a prisoner for twenty-two months, and it was not until three weeks since that I succeeded in making my escape."

"We'll take your story for what it is worth, at present," said the major, "for we can not stop to talk. We must first make some arrangements about obtaining something to eat, and then we must be off."

"My haversack has just been replenished," said the stranger, "and we have sufficient to last us for a day or two, at least."

"Well, let us be moving, then."

The major, as usual, led the way, and Frank walked beside the stranger, who firmly, but respectfully, repelled every attempt he made to enter into conversation, a circumstance which Frank regarded with suspicion.

At length day began to dawn, and the fugitives commenced to cast sidelong glances at their new companion. He was a tall, slimly-built youth, apparently but little older than Frank, and his boyish face wore a look of care and sorrow, which if once seen could never be forgotten, and which showed that, young as he was, his path through life had been any thing but a smooth one. His clothing was reduced almost to tatters; but still there was enough of it left to show that it was "Uncle Sam's blue;" and, as Frank surveyed him from head to foot, he discovered something hanging to one of the shreds of his coat, which immediately interested him in the silent stranger. It was a navy button. This was enough for Frank, who, forgetting the manner in which his advances had been received, inquired:

"Are you a naval officer, sir?"

"Yes," answered the youth, in a low voice, "or, rather, I was once."

"So was I. Give us your hand."

The sad, gloomy look gave way to a smile of genuine pleasure, as the stranger grasped the proffered hand, and shook it heartily.

"What vessel were you attached to, and when and how were you captured?" inquired Frank.

But his companion had relapsed into his former state of gloominess and silence, and seemed to be pondering upon something at once painful and interesting.

Frank made no further attempts to draw him into conversation, and, just as the sun was rising, the major gave the order to halt. He also had noticed the sorrowful look of the young stranger, and, attributing it to a depression of spirits, which any one would feel at finding himself in such circumstances, addressed him, as he came up, with:

"My friend, you appear to be sorely troubled about something. Cheer up; it does no good to be despondent. I know our case is desperate, but it is not altogether hopeless. We do not intend to be recaptured, as long as one of us has strength to draw a trigger."

"I am not troubled about that, sir," answered the youth, throwing himself wearily on the ground. "The cause of my sorrow dates further back than my capture and confinement in prison. I know that I am not the only one who has suffered during this rebellion; but mine is a peculiar case. I have not known a happy day since the war commenced. Every tie that bound me to earth was severed when the first gun was fired on Fort Sumter."

"Ah!" exclaimed Frank, guessing the truth at once. "Then your relatives are rebels."

"Yes, they are; and the most bitter kind of rebels, too. I have kept my secret until I can no longer endure it. I have become completely discouraged, and am greatly in need of what I at first shunned - sympathy. If you will bear with me, I will tell you my circumstances. It will serve to relieve me, and may interest you, and prove that I am really what I profess to be, an escaped prisoner."

"Certainly, let us hear it. Go on," said the major.

Thus encouraged, the youth proceeded:

"My name is George Le Dell; and I am the youngest son of General Le Dell, of the Confederate army. My home is, or rather was, on the Washita River, about ten miles from this very place. When I was seventeen years of age, I was sent North to complete my education, at Yale College, and was just about commencing my senior year, when I received this letter from my father."

Here George paused, and drew from his pocket a bundle of papers, carefully tied up, and, producing a letter, from which the writing was almost obliterated, he handed it to Frank, who read aloud as follows:

CATAHOOLA PARISH, *February* 12, 1861.

MY DEAR GEORGE:

Your letter of the 2d ult. was duly received.

Although your ideas of the civil war, to which you seem to look forward with such anxiety, are rather crude, you are, in the main, correct in your conjectures as to our intentions. Secession is a fixed fact. You know it has often been discussed by our leading men, and the election of Mr. Lincoln has only served to precipitate our action. Had he been defeated, it might have been put off four years longer; but it would be certain to come then. For years the heaven-sanctioned institution of slavery has been subjected to all the attacks that the fiendish imaginations of the Yankee abolitionists could suggest, and we are determined to bear with them no longer. We intend to establish a confederacy of our own, whose corner-stone shall be slavery.

I wish you to come home immediately, as I have secured you a first lieutenant's commission in a cavalry company, which is to be mustered into my regiment. Your brothers have already accepted theirs, and are drilling their companies twice every week. Of course, we do not expect a war, for we have kept the cowardly Yankees under our thumbs so long that they will not dare to oppose us. However, we consider it best to be on the safe side.

Inclosed I send you a check for two hundred dollars, which, I think, will be sufficient to pay all your bills, and to defray your expenses home.

Your mother and sisters send their love.

Hoping to see you soon, and to join hands with you in destroying every vestige of the old Union, I remain,

Yours, affectionately, EDWARD LE DELL.

While Frank was reading this letter, George had sat with his face buried in his hands, not once moving or giving a sign of life: but, as soon as the letter was finished, he raised his pale face, and inquired, in a husky voice:

"What do you think of that? It does not seem possible that a father, who had the least spark of affection for his son, could advise him to follow such a course, does it? Turn the letter over, and you will see a copy of my answer written on the back."

It ran as follows:

YALE COLLEGE, *March* 20, 1861.

## MY DEAR FATHER:

You can not imagine with what feelings of astonishment and sorrow I read your letter of the 12th ult., which was received nearly three weeks since. The reason for my delay in replying you can easily divine. Has it, then, come to this? Is it possible that, in order to do my duty to my country, I must be willing to incur the displeasure of my father? What would you have me do? Assist in pulling down the old flag, and in breaking up the best government the world over saw? Why, father, this is downright madness. I *can not* "join hands" with you in so unholy a cause. On the contrary, as long as that flag needs defenders, you will find me among them. You are deceiving yourself when you say the "cowardly Yankees" will not fight. They are a people "slow to wrath," but they are not cowards, father; and you will find, to your sorrow, that they will resist, to the death, "any and every attempt to alienate any portion of this *Union* from the rest."

Living in the South, as I have, I have long seen this war brewing, but was unwilling to confess it, even to myself; and I had hoped, that if it did come, my father would not countenance it. Why will you do it? You never, never can succeed. The very first attempt you make to withdraw from your allegiance to the United States will be the signal for a war, the like of which the world has never witnessed, and the blood of thousands of men, who will be sacrificed to glut your ambition, will be upon your own heads.

Inclosed, I respectfully return the check, with many thanks for your kindness. I can not use it for the purpose you wish.

Hoping and praying that you and my brothers will consider well before you take the step that will bring you only suffering and disgrace, and will use all your influence to prevent the effusion of blood that must necessarily follow the suicidal course you would pursue, I am, as ever,

Your affectionate son, GEO. LE DELL.

"That was the best I could do at the time," said George, as Frank finished the letter. "I believe I must have been crazy when I wrote it. If I could only have known as much as I do now, I think I could have made a much better plea than that."

"Didn't it have any effect upon your father?" inquired the major.

"Effect!" repeated George. "Yes, it had the effect of making him disinherit and cast me off. Read that," he continued, handing Frank another soiled paper, which looked as though it had been read and thumbed continually. "I felt like one with his death-warrant when I received that."

It ran thus:

CATAHOOLA PARISH, *March* 31, 1861.

SIR:

In reply to your scandalous and insulting letter, I have but a few words to say.

This, then, is the only return you have to make for all the favors I have showered upon you! I had expected great things of you, George, for you have the abilities that would have raised you to a high position in the South; and it seems hard that my fond hopes should be dashed to the ground, by one fell blow, given, too, by your own hand. But I know my duty; and now, sir, I have done with you. I cast you off forever. You will never enter my house again; and not a cent of my property shall ever be possessed by you - no, not even if you were starving. I have instructed my family to forget that such a person as George Le Dell ever existed. Take part with our oppressors, if you choose, but be assured that the justly-merited consequences of your folly will be visited upon you.

In conclusion, I have to say, that if any more letters are received from you, they shall be returned unopened.

EDWARD LE DELL.

"Now you can see exactly how I am situated," said George, taking the letter from Frank's hand, and putting it with the others carefully away in his pocket. "Do you wonder, then, that I am sorrowful, cut off as I am from all my relatives, with strict orders never to cross the threshold of my father's house again, not even if I am dying for want of food? You have, doubtless, heard of the malignity displayed by the rebel leaders toward any Southerner who dares to differ with them in opinion, and have looked upon them as idle stories, gotten up for effect; but I know, by the most bitter experience, that it is a reality. Does it seem possible that a person can be so blind, and act with such cruelty toward a son?

"When the war was fairly begun," he continued, "I kept the vow I had made - that as long as the old flag needed defenders, I should be found among them, by enlisting as fourth master, in what was then called the 'Gun-boat Flotilla,' about to commence operations on the Western waters. I participated in the battle of Island No. 10; was at the taking of Memphis, and at St. Charles; when the 'Mound City' was blown up, I barely escaped being scalded to death. I was on the 'Essex,' when she ran the batteries at Vicksburg, and during the subsequent fight, which resulted in the defeat of the 'Arkansas' ram. About a month after that I was captured with a party of men, while on shore on a foraging expedition. I fought as long as I could, for I knew that death would be preferable to the treatment I should receive; but I was overpowered, and finally surrendered to save the lives of my men. The rebels, of course, immediately commenced crowding about us, and the very first officer I saw was my brother Henry, who had risen to the position of adjutant, in father's regiment. He instantly recognized me, and, after giving strict orders that I should be closely confined, rode off. I had many acquaintances in the regiment. Some of them had been my classmates at college; and the story of my *treason*, as they called it, was given a wide circulation. I fared even worse than I had expected. My food was of the very worst quality, and barely sufficient to sustain life. I was never allowed a shelter of any kind, not even a blanket; and, when my clothing was worn out, I could not obtain another suit. 'Stick to your dirty blue,' said the officer under whose charge I had been placed, 'and every time you look at it, think of the meanness of which you have been guilty.'

"At length, to my relief, the order came for me to be transferred to the prison at Tyler. When I arrived at that place, I was thrust into an old slave-pen, where I was contained nearly twenty months before I succeeded in effecting my escape. I was given to understand that it had been ordered that I was not to be exchanged, but might expect to die a traitor's death at no distant day. Whether or not this was intended to terrify me, I do not know; but, since my escape, I have thought that there were some good grounds for fear; for, during my journey from Tyler to Shreveport, I was not once out of hearing of the blood-hounds that were following my trail. The only support I have had is the consciousness that I have tried to do my duty. If it were not for that, I should be the most miserable person in the world; and I should not care how soon some rebel bullet put an end to my existence.

"Although I am now looked upon by my relatives as a stranger and an outcast, I have determined to visit once more the place which, long ago, I used to call *home*. It is only ten miles from here, and not a step out of our way. Will you accompany me?"

Of course, this strange proposition at first met with strong opposition, especially from the captain. But George assured them that there was not the slightest danger, as all the troops in that part of the country had been ordered to Fort De Russy, and were hourly expecting an attack; consequently they would find no one at home except George's mother, sisters, and a few old negroes who were too feeble to work on the fortifications. Besides as all the troops were now at Red River, their safest course would be to abandon, for awhile, at least, the idea of taking it as their guide to the Mississippi. This silenced their objections, and, after the sentinels for the day had been selected, the fugitives, stretching themselves out on the ground, and fell asleep - all except Frank, who leaned back against a tree. While he kept watch over his sleeping companions, he pondered upon the history of their new acquaintance, and admired the high sense of duty and patriotism that had animated him to make so great a sacrifice for the sake of the "old flag."

# CHAPTER XVII

## THE SCENE AT THE PLANTATION

Next evening, George took the lead, and conducted them through the woods, with a certainty that showed that he was well acquainted with the ground over which they were passing. Not a word did he speak until they emerged from the woods, and found before them a large plantation, with the huge, old-fashioned farm-house, surrounded by its negro quarters and out-buildings, looming up in the distance.

George gazed upon the scene long and earnestly, until his feelings overcame him, when he leaned his head upon his hand, and gave full vent to his sorrow. He did not weep, but the heaving of his chest, and the quivering of his whole frame, showed how severe was the struggle that was going on within him. His companions, who well knew what was passing in his mind, leaned on their weapons, and silently waited until the burst of grief had subsided. At length, George recovered his composure, and said, slowly:

"It looks natural, boys; every thing is just as I left it five years ago. Let us go up to the house. I *must* see my mother and sisters once more. We will say that we are rebel soldiers, and want something to eat. My father and brothers are at Fort De Russy with their commands, so there will be no danger."

"But your uniform," said Frank, anxiously, "that will certainly betray us."

"No danger of that," answered George; "a great many soldiers in the rebel army wear the Federal uniform. There's no danger."

Frank was far from being satisfied, but he fell in with the rest, and followed George toward the house. A few moments' walk brought them to a barn, where they again halted, and, while George stood feasting his eyes on each familiar object, the captain bound the rebel lieutenant hand and foot, and laid him away under a fence-corner; and left him, with the information that his life depended upon his observing the strictest silence. This course was the wisest that could have been adopted, under the circumstances; for it would have been very imprudent to have taken the prisoner with them, as he could easily have found means to make himself known.

George again took the lead, and, when they had almost reached the house, they heard the sound of a piano, and a female voice singing the never-failing "Bonnie Blue Flag."

"There you have it," said George, bitterly; "but don't stop - let's go right in. Major, you had better go up to the door, and ask them to give us something to eat. I dare not trust myself to do it. Be a bitter rebel now, and they will certainly invite us all in, and we will get whatever we ask for. Now, boys," he continued, turning to the others, "don't watch me too closely when we get in the house, or you will betray me."

The major - after making sure that the papers, which had already been of so much service to them, were still in his pocket - ascended the broad stone steps that led up to the portico, and knocked at the door. It was opened by a servant, who, after inquiring what he wanted, led the way into a brilliantly-lighted parlor, where he saw before him George's mother and sisters.

"Good evening, sir," said Mrs. Le Dell, rising from her seat. "Is there any way in which we can serve you?"

The major made known his wants, and a servant was at once dispatched to order supper, and to invite the remainder of the fugitives into the house. As they filed slowly into the room - George bringing up the rear - the particular orders which the major gave about the muskets caused the lady to say:

"You need have no fear, sir. The Yankees have never yet favored us with a visit."

"I know it, ma'am," replied the major, accepting a chair that one of the sisters offered him, "but I have been a soldier so long, that I never omit to make preparations for a fight."

As soon as they were fairly seated, Frank turned to look at George. "That boy must be made of iron," said he to himself, "or else he is among his friends, and we are betrayed;" for, instead of being embarrassed, or wearing his habitual sorrowful look, he sat easily in his chair, and gazed carelessly about the room, as though he were a perfect stranger there, and not a muscle quivered, to show the emotion he really felt, as his eye rested on the familiar faces of his relatives. He calmly met their glances, which Frank thought were directed toward him rather suspiciously, but all attempts to draw him into the conversation that followed, about the war, and the certainty of speedily overpowering the Yankees, and driving them from the land, were unavailing. Once Frank thought he heard one of his sisters whisper, "How much he looks like George!" but he was not recognized, and the supper, which was enlivened by conversation on indifferent subjects, passed off pleasantly.

When the meal was finished, a large bag was filled with provisions, sufficient to last them nearly a week, and given in charge of one of the soldiers; and the major, after thanking the ladies for their kindness, was about to bid them good evening, when there was a clatter of horses' hoofs on the walk, then heavy steps sounded in the hall, and the next moment, to the utter astonishment and horror of the fugitives, three rebel officers entered the room.

They were General Le Dell and his two sons.

Frank's heart fairly came up into his mouth at this unwelcome intrusion, and his first impulse was to draw his revolver and shoot the rebels where they stood; but, on glancing at the major who always seemed to have his wits about him, he abandoned the idea. The major, with the rest, had seized his musket, but, as the rebels entered, he returned it to its place in the corner, (motioning to the others to do the same,) and, saluting the general, said, with a smile:

"I beg your pardon, sir. I did not know but that the Yankees were upon us."

"No danger of that," said the general, with a laugh; "you'll never see them as far up in the country as this. Pray be seated, sir."

After greeting his wife and daughters, the general again turned to the major, whom, by his soldierly bearing, he at once picked out as the leader of the band, and inquired:

"May I ask what you are doing up here? Has not your command been ordered to Fort De Russy?"

"Yes, sir. But I am out on a scout, by order of General Taylor."

"You can have no objection to produce those orders?"

"O no, sir! certainly not. Here they are," answered the major, drawing from his pocket the papers which Frank had captured. The general, after hastily running his eye over them, suddenly exclaimed:

"Why, Lieutenant Somers, how do you do, sir? I am very glad to meet you again. I heard that you had been taken prisoner. I am most happy to see that you have escaped."

This was rather more than the major had been expecting, and

he suddenly found himself placed in a most awkward position. But his presence of mind never forsook him; and, accepting the rebel's proffered hand, he shook it with apparent cordiality, and replied:

"Thank you, sir. I, myself, am not sorry to know that I am a free man once more."

"You probably do not remember me," continued the general, "but I was well acquainted with your father before he moved to Georgia, and used to trot you on my knee when you were a little fellow; and I do believe you were the ugliest little brat I ever had any thing to do with. You did nothing but yell and screech from morning until night. But, by the way, your father met his death in a very singular manner, did he not?"

"Yes, sir - very singular - very singular, indeed," replied the major, promptly, as though he were perfectly familiar with all of the particulars, although in reality he was sorely puzzled to know what to say. What if the rebel should ask him to explain the affair? But the general appeared to be well enough acquainted with the matter, for he continued:

"He died like a brave man, and a soldier. I suppose you intend to take ample revenge upon the Yankees to pay for it."

"Yes, sir; and I am now on the trail of the very man who shot him." The major said this at a venture; but, fortunately, he was correct in his surmise as to the manner in which Mr. Somers departed this life.

While this conversation was going on, Frank was a good deal annoyed to see that George's sisters, and one of his brothers, were engaged in mysterious whisperings, now and then darting suspicious glances toward his new companion. When the general entered, George had risen with the rest and saluted him, after which he had resumed his seat, and the deep blush of excitement that arose to his cheek had quickly given place to the same careless look that Frank had before noticed. George was also aware that the whispering that was going on related to himself, and it was evident that his relatives had some suspicions of who he was; but, if it caused him any uneasiness, he was very careful to conceal it.

At length, one of his brothers drew his chair to his side, and said:

"Excuse me, sir; but I believe I've seen you before."

"I shouldn't be surprised if you had, sir," answered George, steadily meeting the rebel's gaze. "I *know* I've seen you before."

His brother started back in his chair, and a gleam of triumph shot across his face as he exclaimed:

"George, I know you."

"And you will have cause to know me better before this war is over," answered George, forgetting, in his excitement, all the precautions he had before adopted to escape being recognized.

Had a thunderbolt fallen into the room, the astonishment of the general and his wife could not have been greater. They sat in their chairs as motionless as if they had been suddenly turned into stone, gazing at their son as though they could scarcely believe their eyes, while the fugitives sat with their hands on their weapons, wondering what would be the result of George's imprudence. At length the general, who was the first to recover from his astonishment, vociferated:

"You here, you rascal - you young traitor! I thought you were safe in the prison at Tyler again by this time."

"No doubt you did," answered George, bitterly. "But I'm a free man now, and intend to remain so."

"You are free!" repeated the general; "that's a capital joke.

Lieutenant Somers, I charge you with his safe delivery at Tyler."

The major, greatly relieved to find that the general still considered him a rebel, was about to promise that George should be well taken care of, when the latter, to the astonishment of all, boldly declared:

"That is not Lieutenant Somers. These gentlemen are all my friends - Union to the backbone."

"Eh! what?" ejaculated the general, in surprise, scarcely believing what he heard. "These men all Yankees?"

"Yes, sir; every one of them."

"A nice-looking set, surely - a fine lot of jailbirds you are."

"So I have been feeding a lot of tyrants instead of loyal Confederate soldiers," said Mrs. Le Dell, while the sisters gazed at the young hero with contempt pictured in their faces.

"No, mother, you have *not* fed tyrants," answered George, with a good deal of spirit, "but true Union men. It is nothing you need be ashamed of."

"Well, we *are* ashamed of it," said the general, who seemed to be fairly beside himself with rage. "Didn't I tell you never to darken my door again? Where are you traveling to, and what do you intend to do?"

"I am on my way North, and I purpose to join my vessel, if she is still afloat."

"You'll do no such thing. Just consider yourselves prisoners - all of you."

"O no sheneral, I pelieve not," said the captain, quietly, "'cause you see we six been more as you three."

"No, father, we shall never be taken prisoners again - never."

"You are very bold, young man," said the general, who, as he gazed upon the flushed countenance and flashing eyes of his son, could not but admire his courage. "This is big talk for a boy of your age."

"We have already wasted time enough," said the major, growing impatient. "Captain, relieve those gentlemen of their weapons."

The order was promptly obeyed, the rebels offering no resistance.

"Now," resumed the major, "we shall take our leave. Good evening."

"You'll all be in Fort De Russy in less than forty-eight hours," shouted the general, "or I am very much mistaken."

"We'll be dead men, then," answered George. "You will never take us there alive."

The fugitives did not linger to converse, but made all haste to get into the open air. The horses belonging to the rebels, which were found fastened in front of the house, were immediately turned loose, and a thrust from the captain's bayonet sent them galloping up the road.

George silently led the way to the place where they had left their prisoner, and, as soon as he was set at liberty, they bent their steps across the plantation, toward the woods at the rear. Although George had borne up bravely while in the presence of his rebel parents, he could control himself no longer, and tears, which he could not repress, coursed down his cheeks, as ever and anon he turned to take a long, lingering look at the place he could no longer call home. Every emotion he experienced found an echo in the generous heart of Frank, who was scarcely less affected than himself. He could not believe that the scene through which they had just passed was a reality. It did not seem possible that parents could address a son in the language that he had heard used toward George.

The unexpected denouement at the house had rendered the major and captain doubly anxious; for now nothing but the most consummate skill and daring could save them from recapture; and, while the former kept close watch on the house to catch the first sign of pursuit that should be made, the latter gave vent to his feelings by railing, in his broken English, first at George for proposing such an expedition, and then by deprecating his own folly for yielding his consent to it. But there was no help now; regrets could not mend the matter, and nothing but rapid flight could save them.

When they reached the end of the field, George became suddenly aroused. Brushing away the tears that dimmed his eyes, he placed himself at the head of the party, and started on at a rapid pace through the woods.

## CHAPTER XVIII

## ALMOST BETRAYED

Whither he was leading them no one knew, or cared to ask; for, if they had entertained any suspicions in regard to George, the scene at the house had dispelled them; and knowing that he had as much, if not more, cause to dread recapture than themselves, they relied implicitly on him to get them out of their present difficulty.

The woods were pitch-dark, but George seemed to understand what he was about, and, for two hours, not a word was spoken, except, perhaps, now and then a growl of anger, as some one stumbled over a log or bush that lay in his way. Finally, the softness of the ground under their feet indicated that they were approaching a swamp. George now paused, and said:

"Major, with your permission, we will stop here until daylight. It is impossible to go further in this darkness, for it is an ugly road to travel."

"What makes you take to the swamp?" inquired Frank.

"It is a short cut across the country," answered George, "and if we are pursued by blood-hounds we can more easily elude them."

Between sleeping and listening for the noise of pursuit, the fugitives passed the night. As soon as day began to dawn, they made a hasty breakfast on the provisions which they had obtained at the plantation, and resumed their journey. George led the way into the swamp, and, as he seemed to choose the most difficult path, their progress was necessarily slow and laborious. About the middle of the afternoon the swamp became almost impassable, and the major was about to suggest the propriety of picking out an easier path, when George suddenly halted on the banks of a narrow, but deep and sluggish, stream, and, wiping his forehead with his coat-sleeve, said, with something like a sigh of relief:

"Here we are, at last."

"I see we are," said the major, gazing impatiently about on the labyrinth of trees and bushes with which they were surrounded, "but I had rather be almost anywhere else. You might as well get us out of this swamp by the shortest and easiest path you can find."

"I will, if you order me to do so," answered George; "but we are now at as good a harboring place as can be found in a country filled with enemies, bent upon our capture, and thirsting for our blood. I know my father's disposition too well to think that he will allow us to get off easily. The country is fairly overrun with cavalry by this time, and the best thing we can do is to remain here until the excitement has abated a little, and then push for Red River again. That high bank you see over there," he continued, pointing across the stream, "is an island, and all the blood-hounds and negro-hunters in Louisiana would not think of looking for us there. However, I will lead you out of the swamp, if you say so."

After a short consultation, it was decided that it would be best to accept George's plan, as their pursuers would never think of looking for them so near the plantation; and, after divesting themselves of their clothes, they entered the water and struck out for the opposite shore. Frank, who brought up the rear, had scarcely made half a dozen strokes, when he was startled by a loud splashing in the water, followed by a noise resembling the bellowing of a bull, and looked up just in time to see the huge, shining body of an alligator disappear in the muddy water. The utmost horror was depicted on Frank's countenance, as he turned and hastily regained the shore. The others, who were too far out to return, were no less terrified, but they had the presence of mind to retain their hold of their clothing and weapons, and a few hasty strokes brought them to the shore. George and the lieutenant were the only ones who did not seem aware of the danger; for, when the former reached the shore, he proceeded to pull on his clothes, and, seeing Frank standing where he had left him, coolly inquired:

"Why don't you come on? Can't you swim?"

"Yes," answered Frank; "but didn't you see that alligator? I almost ran over him before I saw him."

"O, that's nothing," answered George, carelessly. "If alligators were all we had to fear, we would all be safe at the North in less than two months. They are death on darkeys, but they will not touch a white man in the water, if he keeps moving. There's not the slightest danger. Come on."

Frank was very much inclined to doubt this statement; but, screwing up his courage to the highest pitch, he stepped into the water again, and struck out. When he reached the middle of the stream, he saw a large, black object rise in the water but a short distance from him, and, after regarding him a moment with a pair of small, sharp-looking eyes, it disappeared, with another of those roars which had so startled him but a moment before. He kept on, however, and, in a few moments, reached the shore in safety.

"Now," said George, "there is, or was about five years ago, a cabin on this island, where our negroes used to put up when they came here fishing. Let us see if we can find it."

He commenced leading the way, through the thick bushes and trees, toward the center of the island, and, after a few moments' walk, they suddenly entered a small, clear spot, where stood the cabin of which George had spoken. But a far different scene was presented than they had expected; for a fire was burning near the cabin, and a man stood over it, superintending the cooking of his supper, and conversing in a low tone with a companion who lay stretched out on his blanket close by. Both were dressed in the rebel uniform, and their muskets and a cavalry saber were hung up under the eaves of the cabin. George at once hastily drew back into the bushes, while the captain threw forward his musket, and whispered:

"Major, I pelieve it's petter we shoots them rebels."

Before the major had time to reply, a large dog, which the fugitives had not before noticed, arose from the blanket where he had lain beside his master, and uttered a low growl, whereat the rebels seized their weapons, and were beating a precipitate retreat, when a loud "halt!" from the major brought them to a stand-still.

"We takes you all two brisoners," said the captain, as he advanced from the bushes, followed by the remainder of the fugitives, who all held their weapons in readiness. "Drop them guns."

The rebels did as they were ordered, and the major said:

"Now we will talk to you. Who and what are you?"

The men hesitated for a moment, and at length one of them, turning to his companion with a meaning look, said:

"We're caught, any way we can fix it, Jim, and we may as well make a clean breast of it. We are deserters."

"What are you doing here?"

"We came here to get out of the way of you fellows who were sent after us. It is as good a place of refuge as we could find, and, to tell the truth, we did not think you would discover it. You must have followed us with blood-hounds."

"No, sir; we did not," exclaimed the major, indignantly. "What do you take us for - savages?"

"Well, you found us in some way," replied the rebel, "and I suppose we're done for."

"No, not necessarily. We shall not trouble you as long as you behave yourselves, for we are in a bad fix also."

"Are you deserters, too?" inquired the rebel, joyfully. "If you are, we are all right, for, with the force we have, we can defend this island against as many men as they can pile into Louisiana. But, shoot me if I didn't think you were looking after us. I see you have gobbled a Yankee," he continued, pointing to the lieutenant. "But, come, sit down and have some supper."

The major was perfectly willing that the rebels should consider themselves in the presence of their own men; and, besides, if they were really deserters, their being on the island proved what George had told them, that it was considered to be a safe place for concealment. The only cause he had for uneasiness was the presence of the rebel lieutenant; if he should find opportunity to talk to the men, he would soon make known the true state of affairs.

"Captain," he whispered, turning to that individual, "keep an eye on that prisoner of ours, and do not, under any circumstances, leave him alone with these deserters."

The fugitives then threw themselves on the ground, under the shade of the trees, and, while the majority readily entered into conversation with the rebels, Frank, who had grown suspicious of every thing that looked like friendship, in spite of the cordial manner with which the deserters had welcomed them, could not, for a long time, satisfy himself that every thing was right. However, as he could detect nothing in the actions of the men to confirm his suspicions, and, as the fact that their food was supplied to them by a negro, who visited the island every night, gave him good grounds for believing that there *might*, after all, be some truth in their statement, he dismissed the subject for the present, but determined that the men should be closely watched.

During the two following days, which the fugitives spent on the island, nothing suspicious was discovered. Wherever the lieutenant went he was closely followed by his keeper, and he was never allowed to be alone with the other rebels. In fact, he did not seem at all desirous of having any conversation with them, for, with the exception of taking a short walk about the island after every meal, he passed both day and night in dozing in the cabin. The rebels, on the other hand, appeared to believe him a "Yankee," and as such, considered him beneath their notice. Frank was beginning to think that his fears had been utterly groundless, when, on the third night, he was fortunate enough to detect a plot, which, if carried into execution, would have put an end to all his hopes of seeing home again, perhaps forever.

It was his duty to stand sentry from dark until midnight. As he walked his beat, listening for the signal of the negro, whom he every moment expected with another supply of provisions, and thinking over the scenes through which he had passed since he had entered the service, he heard a slight rustling in the bushes back of the cabin, and saw one of the deserters disappear among the trees. What could the man mean by moving about the island at that time of night? There must be something wrong, for his stealthy movements proved that he did not wish to be observed. While Frank was pondering upon the subject, and debating the propriety of informing the major of the fact, the lieutenant sauntered leisurely up to the place where he was standing, and, stretching his arms, languidly inquired:

"Don't you think it is very sultry this evening? It is impossible for me to sleep."

This was something unusual for the lieutenant, who, although he had often conversed very freely with the major, had never before spoken to Frank since the night of his capture. The latter knew that the rebel had some object in view, and at once determined to act as though he suspected nothing, and to await the issue of affairs.

"Yes, it is very warm," he replied, fanning himself with his cap. "I shall be glad when I get North again."

"No doubt of it," answered the rebel, carelessly. "I believe I'll go down to the spring and get a cup of water, if you have no objections."

As soon as he had disappeared, Frank threw himself on his hands and knees, and crawling to the edge of the bank, looked over, and saw the lieutenant and the deserter, whom he had seen stealing from the cabin, engaged in conversation.

"They will be here to-morrow night, then, without fail?" he heard the lieutenant ask.

"Yes, so the negro says," replied the deserter.

"Twelve of them, did you say? That will make sixteen, including the negro. There will be none too many of us, for these Yankees will fight like perfect demons. If we fail, our lives will not be worth five minutes' purchase."

"Do not have any fears," replied the other. "I have made 'assurance doubly sure,' and failure is impossible."

"Well, go back to the cabin now," said the lieutenant, "for you might be missed."

On hearing this, Frank hastily retreated, and regained his post. Presently the lieutenant returned, and, after giving Frank a drink of water from his cup, sought his blanket.

"A pretty piece of business, indeed," thought Frank, as he commenced walking his beat again. "It is fortunate I discovered it. I'll keep a lookout for the negro, and learn all I can from him."

He was not obliged to wait long, for presently a low whistle, that sounded from the opposite side of the bayou, told that the negro was in waiting. Frank answered the signal, when a light canoe shot out from the shore and approached the island. In a few moments the negro walked up the bank, and, depositing a large bag of provisions in the cabin, turned to go back, followed by Frank, who commenced conversation by observing, "A warm evening, uncle;" but, the moment they were out of sight of the cabin, he inquired, in a low voice:

"Are those twelve men all ready to come here to-morrow night?"

"Sar! what twelve men?" asked the negro, in well-feigned surprise. "I dunno nuffin 'bout no twelve men."

"O, now, see here, uncle," said Frank, "that story won't do at all, for I know better than that. You see this is the first chance I have had to talk to you, for these Yanks watch me so closely. Now, at what hour are they to be here?"

"I tol' you, massa," repeated the negro, "dat I dunno nuffin 'bout no men;" and, thinking he had settled the matter, turned to walk away.

But Frank was not yet done with him, and, seeing that he was too cunning to be "pumped," determined to try what effect the sight of his weapons would produce. Seizing the negro by the collar, he pressed the muzzle of his revolver against his head, whispering, between his clenched teeth:

"See here, you black rascal! you *do* know all about the matter, for you have carried orders from these rebels here to their friends. So, confess the whole truth, instantly."

"I dunno nuffin 'bout no men, I tol' you," persisted the negro.

"You won't confess, eh?" said Frank, cocking his revolver. "Then you're a dead man."

"O Lor'! don't shoot, massa," exclaimed the now terrified negro. "What shall I 'fess."

"Confess the truth," replied Frank, "and you shall not be harmed; but, if you try to deceive me, you're a dead darkey. Answer such questions as I shall ask you. In the first place, who are these men who say they are rebel deserters?"

"One of 'em is my massa, an' de other is a captain in de army."

"What are they doing on this island?"

"Dey come here for to cotch young massa George Le Dell, 'cause dey knowed he would be shore for to come here."

"Well, how many men are you going to bring over here to-morrow night?"

"Twelve, sar, an' I fotch 'em in de big canoe."

"At what hour?"

"Midnight, when de moon hab gone down, an' my massa is on guard."

Having got this important information, Frank released the negro, and regained his post without being discovered. At midnight he called his relief, and then lay down on the ground and fell asleep.

After breakfast, the next morning, as the major went to the spring to fill his cup, Frank, who had followed close behind him, said suddenly:

"We're in trouble again."

"Yes, and always shall be," answered the major, coolly, "until we are safe at the North. But what is the matter now - any thing new?"

"Yes," replied Frank, speaking in a whisper, lest he should be overheard. "Last night I discovered that there is a plot on foot to recapture us, and the attempt is to be made at midnight. These men we found here are not deserters, as they claim to be, but still belong to the army."

The major, as if not at all concerned, raised the cup to his lips and slowly drained it, keeping his eyes fastened on Frank, who finally began to grow impatient, and inquired:

"What shall we do to defeat them?"

"Keep cool, for one thing," answered the major. "But tell me all the particulars."

Frank then recounted every thing that had transpired. When he had finished, the major carelessly remarked:

"The rascals played their parts pretty well; in fact, very well, indeed. Now, the first thing to be done is to go back to the camp and secure those two fellows. We'll determine upon our plans afterward."

They accordingly slowly returned to the cabin, and found their men engaged, one in sharpening his Bowie-knife, and the other cleaning his rifle. The major walked straight up to one of them, and, seizing his musket, wrested it from him. The other, comprehending the state of affairs in an instant, exclaimed "Betrayed!" and turned to run, when Frank grappled with him and threw him to the ground.

"What ish the matter here, any way?" exclaimed the captain, who was taken so completely by surprise that he stood riveted

Harry Castlemon

to the spot.

"Lend a hand here," answered Frank, struggling desperately with his man, "and ask your questions afterward."

The captain at once sprang to Frank's assistance; in a moment, the rebel was disarmed, and his hands bound behind his back. The major, in the mean time, having succeeded in securing his man, gave a hasty explanation of the matter, and ended by saying:

"There is but one way for us to do, and that is to leave this place at once. Tie those two rebels to some of these trees, and then we'll be off."

As soon as this was accomplished, and the major had satisfied himself that there was not the least chance for their escape, he said:

"Now, we shall leave you here. Your friends will probably be along at midnight and liberate you."

The rebels made no reply, and the fugitives, after collecting their weapons, again set out, taking the lieutenant with them. The major ordered George to lead them by the most direct route to Red River. This was a desperate measure, but their case was also desperate. The country on all sides of them had been alarmed, and, if Red River was closely guarded, the Washita was equally dangerous.

So anxious were they to put as long a distance as possible between them and the scene of their late narrow escape, that they traveled until the next morning - stopping only to eat sparingly of some provisions which one of the soldiers had secured before leaving the island - and then camped in the swamp, and slept soundly.

# CHAPTER XIX

## CONCLUSION

The next evening, as soon as it was dark, they again started out. For three days they held their course straight through the woods, and, finally, releasing their prisoner, they bent their steps toward Red River, where, after many delays, they succeeded in securing a canoe.

They traveled entirely by night, and, in a short time reached Alexandria, where they landed just above the village, and went ashore to reconnoiter. To their disappointment they found that the place was filled with soldiers, and that a pontoon-bridge had been thrown across the river, and was guarded at both ends.

After making all their observations, they retreated to the bank of the river, and held a consultation. Should they abandon their canoe, and strike off through the woods again? There were many objections to this plan. The country, for miles around, was, doubtless, filled with encampments, and guarded by pickets, and their progress would involve both danger and difficulty. Besides, they were almost worn out with travel and constant watching, and, even had there been no obstacles in their way, it would have been impossible for them to sustain a long journey across the country. It was finally decided to follow the river. They resolved to run the bridge, and hoped, aided by darkness, to escape discovery. It was necessary that some one should guide the  canoe, and, as Frank perfectly understood its management, he was selected for the purpose.

As soon as the moon had gone down, Frank seated himself in the stern of the canoe, and his companions stretched themselves out under the thwarts, as much out of sight as possible. As soon as all was ready, he moved their frail craft from the shore, with one silent sweep of the paddle, turning it toward the bridge.

It was a dangerous undertaking; but Frank although perfectly aware of this, and knowing what his fate would be if he was recaptured, had never been more cool and self-possessed in his life. He remained at his station until they were within a hundred yards of the bridge. He then drew in his paddle, and laid on the bottom of the canoe, with the others, awaiting the issue.

Propelled by the force of the current, the canoe rapidly approached the bridge, and, presently, they could distinctly hear the sentinels talking with each other. They had not been expecting an enemy in that quarter; but, in a few moments, that danger was passed. For miles below Alexandria, the river was lined with picket fires, and the slightest noise would have betrayed them. But they were not discovered; and, after a week's journey - during which the papers Frank had taken from the rebel lieutenant procured them food - they reached the Mississippi River.

To their disappointment they learned that Vicksburg was still in possession of the rebels, and that they had two hundred miles further to go before they would be among friends again. After having come so far, they could not be discouraged, but, taking a few moments' repose, they again set out.

The current in the river was very strong, and it was a month before they reached Vicksburg. One dark night, they ran by the city in safety, and the next morning, to their joy, they found themselves in sight of a gun-boat, for which they immediately shaped their course. As they approached her,

Frank thought there was something about the vessel that looked familiar; and when they came alongside, he found that it was the Ticonderoga. She had been repainted, and some of her rigging altered, which was the reason he had not recognized her before.

Frank almost cried with joy when he found himself once more on his own ship; and all the dangers he had undergone were forgotten in a moment. He saw many new officers on board, and a master's mate met them at the gangway, who, probably, held the position he once occupied.

The captain stood on deck, but did not recognize him; and even the old mate, with whom Frank had been an especial favorite, gazed at him as though he were a perfect stranger.

"Walk up on deck, men," said the officer who received them, and who, doubtless, took them for rebel deserters, "the captain wants to see you."

Frank led the way up the ladder, and as they filed, one after the other, on to the quarter-deck, the captain inquired:

"Where do you belong, men?"

"I formerly belonged here, sir," answered Frank, raising his hat; "and I have the honor to report myself on board."

"Report yourself on board!" repeated the captain, in a tone of surprise.

"Yes, sir. I haven't been on board since we were down Yazoo Pass. I did not intend to remain away so long, when I left the ship, but I couldn't help it."

"Explain yourself," said the captain, growing impatient; "I don't know what you mean."

"My name is Nelson, sir; I was captured at" -

"Why, Mr. Nelson!" exclaimed the captain, seizing his hand with a grip that almost wrung from him a cry of pain, "is it possible this is you? I never expected to see you again. But who are these with you?"

"They are some of our soldiers, whom I met on the way down."

Their story was very soon told. When it became known that the rebel lieutenant who was talking with the captain was none other than Frank Nelson, the quarter-deck was filled with officers and men, who gathered around the young hero, congratulating him on his safe return. He was compelled to relate the particulars of his escape over and over again; and, finally, he and his companions were taken down into the wardroom, and supplied with clothing more befitting their stations than that which they wore.

For two days Frank did nothing but answer questions and relate incidents that occurred during the flight from Shreveport. But at length the reaction came, and he, with several of his companions, were seized with the fever. For a month Frank was very ill; but he received the best of care, and, aided by his strong constitution, the progress of the disease was stayed.

One day the captain came into his room, and, seating himself by his bedside, inquired:

"Well, Mr. Nelson, how do you prosper?"

"Oh, I am getting along finely, thank you, sir."

"Do you think you will be strong enough to travel, soon?"

"Yes, sir," answered Frank, wondering what made the captain ask that question.

"How would you enjoy a trip home?"

"Oh, I should enjoy it above all things, sir I never was away from home so long before, in my life."

"Well," said the captain, as he rose to go, "you must hurry and get well as fast as you can. The doctor told me that he thought you ought to go North and recruit a little; so I wrote to the Admiral, and obtained you a sick-leave. The dispatch boat will be along in a day or two, and I will send you up the river on her. I think it is nothing more than right that you should go home for a couple of months, at least, for you have been through a good deal for a young man of your age."

The thought that he was soon to see his home again did Frank more good than all the medicine the doctor had given him; and, by the time the mail steamer arrived, he was able to walk about. In two weeks they arrived at Cairo. The steamer had scarcely touched the wharf-boat before Archie, who had seen his cousin standing on deck, sprang on board.

We can not describe the meeting. To Archie it was like finding one risen from the dead; for he had heard of Frank's capture, and had never expected to see him again. A multitude of questions were asked and answered on both sides; and when Frank informed Archie that he was on his way home, the latter abruptly left him, and hurried to the fleet paymaster to ask permission to accompany his cousin. This, as business was dull, and as Archie had always been very faithful, was readily obtained. They made preparations for immediate departure. After Archie had telegraphed to his father that Frank was safe - taking care, however, not to say one word about their coming home - they took their seats in the cars, and soon arrived safely in Portland. Frank remained there only one day, and then set out for Lawrence.

Only those who have been in similar circumstances can imagine what Frank's feelings were, as he stood on the deck of the Julia Burton, and found himself once more in sight of his native village. Familiar objects met his eye on every side. There were the weeds that surrounded the perch-bed, where he, in company with George and Harry Butler, was fishing when he made the acquaintance of Charles Morgan, who was afterward the leader of the Regulators. Above the perch-bed was the bass-ground, and to the left was Reynard's Island, where the black fox had been captured. Near the middle of the river lay Strawberry Island, which had been the silent witness of many a sailing match between the yachts of the village; in short, every thing looked exactly as it did when, just fifteen months before, he had sailed down the river on that same steamer, on his way to Portland.

As soon as the steamer was made fast to the wharf, Frank gave his trunk in charge of a drayman, and set out on foot for the cottage; for, impatient as he was to get home, he wished to have time to enjoy the sight of each familiar object along the road; besides, he wished to come in upon his folks (who little dreamed that he was so near to) suddenly, and take them by surprise. Every thing in the village, and along the road, looked as natural as ever; not a tree, bush, or stump seemed to have been removed. At length he reached the bend in the road which brought him in sight of his home. He stopped to gaze upon the scene. Not a thing about the house or orchard had been changed. He noticed that a part of the rose-bush which covered his window, and which had been broken off in a storm the night before he left, still swung loose in the wind; and even his fish-pole, which he had hung up under the eaves of his museum, had not been touched.

While he stood thus, trying in vain to choke back the tears, he was aroused by a well-known bark; the next moment Brave bounded over the fence, and came toward his master at the top of his speed. He had been lying in his accustomed place in front of the house; he had seen Frank approaching, and had recognized him in an instant. Frank wound his arms around the faithful animal's neck, and, after caressing him for a moment, again started toward the house, Brave leading the way, with every demonstration of joy. As soon as Frank succeeded in quieting him, he walked through the gate, noiselessly opened the door leading into the hall, and paused to listen.

He heard Julia's voice singing one of his favorite songs, while a loud clatter of dishes told him that Hannah was still in charge of the kitchen.

Brave ran into the sitting-room, barking and whining furiously, and Frank heard his mother say:

"Julia, I guess you did not close the front door when you came in. Be quiet, Brave. What is the matter with you?" and Mrs. Nelson, dressed in deep mourning, came into the hall. The next moment she was clasped in her son's arms.

\*　　\*　　\*　　\*　　\*

Let those who have sons and brothers in the service imagine the joy that prevailed in that house! They had heard of Frank's capture, through Archie and the captain of the Ticonderoga, and, afterward, that he was killed at Shreveport, while attempting to run by the guards.

"Mother," said Frank, as soon as the greeting was over, "you told me, when I went away, never to shrink from my duty, but always to do what was required of me, no matter what the danger might be. Have I obeyed your instructions?"

Reader, will you answer the question for her? and will you follow Frank through his adventures before Vicksburg and on the Lower Mississippi?

# Choose from Thousands of 1stWorldLibrary Classics By

A. M. Barnard
Ada Leverson
Adolphus William Ward
Aesop
Agatha Christie
Alexander Aaronsohn
Alexander Kielland
Alexandre Dumas
Alfred Gatty
Alfred Ollivant
Alice Duer Miller
Alice Turner Curtis
Alice Dunbar
Ambrose Bierce
Amelia E. Barr
Amory H. Bradford
Andrew Lang
Andrew McFarland Davis
Andy Adams
Anna Sewell
Annie Besant
Annie Hamilton Donnell
Annie Payson Call
Annonaymous
Anton Chekhov
Arnold Bennett
Arthur Conan Doyle
Arthur M. Winfield
Arthur Ransome
Atticus
B.H. Baden-Powell
B. M. Bower
Baroness Emmuska Orczy
Baroness Orczy
Basil King
Bayard Taylor
Ben Macomber
Bertha Muzzy Bower
Bjornstjerne Bjornson
Booth Tarkington
Boyd Cable
Bram Stoker
C. Collodi
C. E. Orr
C. M. Ingleby
Carolyn Wells
Catherine Parr Traill
Charles A. Eastman
Charles Dickens

Charles Dudley Warner
Charles Farrar Browne
Charles Ives
Charles Kingsley
Charles Klein
Charles Amory Beach
Charles Hanson Towne
Charles Lathrop Pack
Charles Whibley
Charles Willing Beale
Charlotte M. Braeme
Charlotte M. Yonge
Charlotte Perkins Stetson
Clair W. Hayes
Clarence Day Jr.
Clarence E. Mulford
Clemence Housman
Confucius
Cornelis DeWitt Wilcox
Cyril Burleigh
D. H. Lawrence
Daniel Defoe
David Garnett
Dinah Craik
Don Carlos Janes
Donald Keyhoe
Dorothy Kilner
Dougan Clark
Douglas Fairbanks
E. Nesbit
E.P.Roe
E. Phillips Oppenheim
Earl Barnes
Edgar Rice Burroughs
Edith Van Dyne
Edith Wharton
Edward J. O'Biren
Edward S. Ellis
Edwin L. Arnold
Eleanor Atkins
Eliot Gregory
Elizabeth Gaskell
Elizabeth McCracken
Elizabeth Von Arnim
Ellem Key
Emerson Hough
Emilie F. Carlen
Emily Dickinson
Enid Bagnold

Enilor Macartney Lane
Erasmus W. Jones
Ernie Howard Pie
Ethel Turner
Ethel Watts Mumford
Eugenie Foa
Eugene Wood
Eustace Hale Ball
Evelyn Everett-green
Everard Cotes
F. H. Cheley
F. J. Cross
Federick Austin Ogg
Ferdinand Ossendowski
Francis Bacon
Francis Darwin
Frances Hodgson Burnett
Frances Parkinson Keyes
Frank Gee Patchin
Frank Harris
Frank Jewett Mather
Frank L. Packard
Frank V. Webster
Frederic Stewart Isham
Frederick Trevor Hill
Frederick Winslow Taylor
Friedrich Kerst
Friedrich Nietzsche
Fyodor Dostoyevsky
G.A. Henty
G.K. Chesterton
Gabrielle E. Jackson
Garrett P. Serviss
Gaston Leroux
George A. Warren
George Ade
Geroge Bernard Shaw
George Durston
George Ebers
George Eliot
George Gissing
George MacDonald
George Meredith
George Orwell
George Sylvester Viereck
George Tucker
George W. Cable
George Wharton James
Gertrude Atherton

Grace E. King
Grace Gallatin
Grant Allen
Guillermo A. Sherwell
Gulielma Zollinger
Gustav Flaubert
H. A. Cody
H. B. Irving
H.C. Bailey
H. G. Wells
H. H. Munro
H. Irving Hancock
H. Rider Haggard
H. W. C. Davis
Hamilton Wright Mabie
Hans Christian Andersen
Harold Avery
Harold McGrath
Harriet Beecher Stowe
Harry Houidini
Helent Hunt Jackson
Helen Nicolay
Hendrik Conscience
Hendy David Thoreau
Henri Barbusse
Henrik Ibsen
Henry Adams
Henry Ford
Henry Frost
Henry James
Henry Jones Ford
Henry Seton Merriman
Henry W Longfellow
Herbert A. Giles
Herbert N. Casson
Herman Hesse
Homer
Honore De Balzac
Horace Walpole
Horatio Alger Jr.
Howard Pyle
Howard R. Garis
Hugh Lofting
Hugh Walpole
Humphry Ward
Ian Maclaren
Inez Haynes Gillmore
Irving Bacheller
Israel Abrahams
Ivan Turgenev
J.G.Austin

J. Henri Fabre
J. M. Barrie
J. Macdonald Oxley
J. S. Fletcher
J. S. Knowles
J. Storer Clouston
Jack London
Jacob Abbott
James Allen
James Andrews
James Baldwin
James DeMille
James Joyce
James Lane Allen
James Lane Allen
James Oliver Curwood
James Oppenheim
James Otis
James R. Driscoll
Jane Austen
Janet Aldridge
Jens Peter Jacobsen
Jerome K. Jerome
John Burroughs
John Cournos
John F. Kennedy
John Gay
John Glasworthy
John Habberton
John Joy Bell
John Kendrick Bangs
John Milton
John Philip Sousa
Jonas Lauritz Idemil Lie
Jonathan Swift
Joseph A. Altsheler
Joseph Carey
Joseph Conrad
Joseph E. Badger Jr
Joseph Hergesheimer
Joseph Jacobs
Jules Vernes
Julian Hawthrone
Julie A Lippmann
Justin Huntly McCarthy
Kakuzo Okakura
Kenneth Grahame
Kenneth McGaffey
Kate Langley Bosher
Kate Langley Bosher
Katherine Cecil Thurston

Katherine Stokes
L. A. Abbot
L. T. Meade
L. Frank Baum
Latta Griswold
Laura Lee Hope
Laurence Housman
Lawrence Beasley
Leo Tolstoy
Leonid Andreyev
Lewis Carroll
Lewis Sperry Chafer
Lilian Bell
Lloyd Osbourne
Louis Hughes
Louis Tracy
Louisa May Alcott
Lucy Fitch Perkins
Lucy Maud Montgomery
Lydia Miller Middleton
Lyndon Orr
M. Corvus
M. H. Adams
Margaret E. Sangster
Margaret Vandercook
Margret Penrose
Maria Edgeworth
Maria Thompson Daviess
Mariano Azuela
Marion Polk Angellotti
Mark Overton
Mark Twain
Mary Austin
Mary Catherine Crowley
Mary Cole
Mary Hastings Bradley
Mary Roberts Rinehart
Mary Rowlandson
M. Wollstonecraft Shelley
Maud Lindsay
Max Beerbohm
Myra Kelly
Nathaniel Hawthrone
Nicolo Machiavelli
O. F. Walton
Oscar Wilde
Owen Johnson
P.G. Wodehouse
Paul and Mabel Thorne
Paul G. Tomlinson
Paul Severing

Percy Brebner
Peter B. Kyne
Plato
R. Derby Holmes
R. L. Stevenson
R. S. Ball
Rabindranath Tagore
Rahul Alvares
Ralph Bonehill
Ralph Henry Barbour
Ralph Victor
Ralph Waldo Emmerson
Rene Descartes
Rex Beach
Rex E. Beach
Richard Harding Davis
Richard Jefferies
Richard Le Gallienne
Robert Barr
Robert Frost
Robert Gordon Anderson
Robert L. Drake
Robert Lansing
Robert Lynd
Robert Michael Ballantyne
Robert W. Chambers
Rosa Nouchette Carey
Rudyard Kipling
Samuel B. Allison

Samuel Hopkins Adams
Sarah Bernhardt
Sarah C. Hallowell
Selma Lagerlof
Sherwood Anderson
Sigmund Freud
Standish O'Grady
Stanley Weyman
Stella Benson
Stephen Crane
Stewart Edward White
Stijn Streuvels
Swami Abhedananda
Swami Parmananda
T. S. Ackland
T. S. Arthur
The Princess Der Ling
Thomas A. Janvier
Thomas A Kempis
Thomas Anderton
Thomas Bailey Aldrich
Thomas Bulfinch
Thomas De Quincey
Thomas H. Huxley
Thomas Hardy
Thomas More
Thornton W. Burgess
U. S. Grant
Valentine Williams

Various Authors
Vaughan Kester
Victor Appleton
Virginia Woolf
Walter Camp
Walter Scott
Washington Irving
Wilbur Lawton
Wilkie Collins
Willa Cather
Willard F. Baker
William Dean Howells
William le Queux
W. Makepeace Thackeray
William W. Walter
Winston Churchill
Yei Theodora Ozaki
Yogi Ramacharaka
Young E. Allison
Zane Grey